MURDER FOR A SONG

MUSICAL MAYHEM
BOOK ONE

KM JACKWAYS

OLD SOULS PRESS

CHAPTER 1

"Are you ready to be famous?" Esther's friend leaned in as he went past.

"Hardly famous. It's an aged care home," she reminded Ashton, as he stepped up to the till, and pressed a few buttons and the cash drawer opened.

And no, Esther thought. *No, I'm not.* Tomorrow night was their first proper gig, and every time she thought of it, her stomach roiled with nausea. She focused on the chill beats of Pink Floyd, coming through her earpods, to quiet her mind, and went back to flicking through the books. One of the guitar music books had sold in the last fortnight, and two of the beginner piano lesson books. She sighed, pulled some extra stock from her bag and tucked them into the gaps.

Esther stood up and stretched, looking over the

shelves. Her sweater felt too thick. It would be good to get out of the stuffy shop.

Book Ends was a ridiculously large shop for a small town such as Ledstow. The old town lodge was reformed into a glorious shop for booklovers. The dark pink carpet from the '70's was threadbare underfoot in places, and huge stained glass lightshades hung from the ceiling. With a dark wood bar that had been transformed into the counter, it was pure cosy kitsch. The new books were neatly stacked in shelves around the edges of the room and second hand books covered two long tables. People were reading in huge, tatty armchairs next to the fireplace. The booths were reading nooks, each with a different theme.

Sometimes, she imagined the people who had hitched their horses outside, fed and watered there, who had laughed and schemed and loved. The feeling of a haven for weary travellers remained in the strong wooden bones.

Esther loved coming here to merchandise the stock, especially because she got to hang out with her friend. Behind the till, Ashton raised his eyebrows at her when he saw her pop up. He was counting the coins into piles, but gave her a grin.

Down the front of the shop, Rochelle was frantically stacking Christmas books on the display table, the neck of her shirt darkened with sweat. Her candy cane earrings bobbed as she opened picture books to stand them up, inviting little fingers to flick through and eyes to drink in the colourful images. Jayden started hammering a new shelf support in and Esther cringed with each hollow crack.

She looked at her two shelves with a critical eye. The problem was that music theory books weren't that sexy. It needed *something*. She reached for the sign, pulled the centrepiece out and slipped in a piece of paper for 25% off — as if that would make all the difference. A discount and something topical, perhaps. She propped up Modern Carols for Millennials onto the stand beside it. Her boss at the music shop surely wouldn't mind.

"Alright everyone, let's get out of here." Rochelle bellowed. "We're already running late to get home. You're on your own time now." The former parking warden put her hands on her hips and glared at them all in turn.

Esther popped out her earpods and the chaos rushed back in. The slide and chink of the coins in a regular rhythm, the low-level carols in the background and a truck whooshing past on the road outside.

"Nearly there," Ashton said to her, without pausing in his counting. "Good takings today."

Rochelle popped up behind her. "Busy, though. And it's only going to get worse. Turn the music off for me, will you? And check on the computer if we've got any copies of 'A Brief History of Ledstow and Surrounds' in the store."

"Sure." Esther went round the bar and flicked the stereo off, then tapped on the keyboard. "By Moran O'Malley? Should be two copies. It's 500 pages, so I'm not sure about the brief part," she added.

"Alright, just note it down on a piece of paper. Vicky got an online order." Ashton caught her eye, as she wrote it on a sticky note and pressed it onto the edge of the computer. They always laughed about the terrible systems in the shop.

"What the hell, Mr Deed?" Rochelle held her hand out for the book. The customer was sitting in the kids' corner. It was painted as a garden, complete with mushroom seats and a tree branch that you could hang off, and they had started selling toys too. Esther thought this area was an inspired idea and she was sure it was the reason the shop did so well. "Didn't you hear me announce that the shop was closing soon" — she looked at her watch — "twenty minutes ago?"

"Oh, I am sorry," Harry Deed said. He stood there for a moment patting his pockets, until he obviously found his keys, then let himself out the front door. Rochelle checked the lock again, behind him.

"Don't you all want to get back to your families?" Rochelle stood by the door to the back room, near the stacks of boxes of holiday-themed books that had to be unpacked, and gestured with her arms as if to herd them all out.

"Phoebe," Rochelle said, as a young woman who was sweating profusely, came around the corner and stopped in the doorway. "You're a bit early. I haven't managed to get the boxes out of your way yet."

Phoebe plucked at her navy pinny. "I know, I'm so sorry," she said. "I wanted to get the cleaning finished early so I could have dinner with my mum. She's just arrived in town," she said, talking over the heads of the others, who were grabbing their bags and filing out the door.

"Don't make a habit of it, then," Rochelle said.

Phoebe pressed herself against the doorway as Ashton passed through. "I won't."

"Merry Christmas, losers," he called with a wave. "See you on the other side."

"I'll see you tomorrow," Esther said to him. She waited under the eaves.

"We are going to knock their socks off," he said, over his shoulder.

False teeth, more like, Esther thought, but she gave him a smile.

The fog seemed to swirl and turn in the alleyway as they hurried through. As they stepped out into the town square, Rochelle turned to her.

"Can you help out on Christmas Eve, Esther? It's

going to be hectic without Ashton there. I don't know why he took his leave the week before the busiest time of the year. Honestly, it's like herding cats at the shop sometimes."

"Oh, ah," she said, desperately thinking of an excuse, and coming up short. She looked around her, and noticed two policemen across the road, stopping to talk to someone. Nothing that inspired any great excuse. She shrugged. Rochelle knew she had nothing on and no partner to go home to. "Well, not really…"

"Alright." Rochelle's tone was defensive. "It's your choice, of course."

Esther immediately felt guilty. But why should she? She didn't *have* to come in and do extra hours, after all. At the corner, Esther said goodbye and stepped out onto the road. She must have still been thinking about it, because wind whooshed past her nose.

"Careful!"

She jumped back just in time, as a cyclist came screaming down the hill out of the fog and whipped past.

"Are you alright?"

Rochelle patted Esther on the back while she took a few big breaths. "You give that kitten a big hug when you get home. And maybe hop online and buy a lotto ticket," she added.

"Yeah," she said, shakily. At least her flat was just around the corner.

Esther looked twice this time and crossed the road, pulling her coat around her. She was so busy looking side to side that she almost tripped over a man who was lying on the footpath on the other side outside the shops.

"Mmm," he mumbled. She looked down at the two pairs of fingerless gloves he was wearing. He must be freezing. She fumbled in her wallet and dropped a five pound note into his jar.

"Mm… Merry Christmas!" he called after her, as she hurried off.

When she got home to her flat, she still felt on edge. A rasping whisper came from somewhere nearby, and she gritted her teeth. A bird took flight from the fence, wings beating. *Get a grip*, she thought.

With shaky fingers, she let herself into the flat. Something shiny sitting in the middle of the floor caught her eye. What had been a golden bauble, but was now a bird's nest of tinsel and a white polystyrene ball, was sitting in the entranceway.

She followed an increasingly chaotic and sparkly trail of destruction into the lounge, where the Christmas tree was lying on its side. On the couch, with a strand of glittery gold trailing from beneath him, the grey kitten was sleeping in a tiny ball, oozing innocence from every silver hair.

Esther heaved a sigh and went over to the cat, stroking its fluffy body.

"You've got a feather here, too, Louis," she said. "What have you been up to?"

In response, he stretched out a paw in front and, tiny claws extended, kneaded into the fabric of the couch. Esther winced when the material got stuck in his paws. She had only just finished paying the couch off, and every thread of that thing was valuable.

She heated up a supermarket pizza and sat on the kitchen stool to eat it. The cat twirled around beneath her, mewing, and eyeing her as if she was the absolute worst owner in the world.

"What have I forgotten, Louis?" She wiggled her nose, which was itching, then reached for her antihistamines. "I better take these, or I won't be able to snuggle you." She reached for his tinned food. "It's not this you're after, is it?" The cat gave her a foul look, until she scooped some into his bowl.

Esther got ready for bed, and with a last glance at the chaos on the floor, she turned out the light, picking up the kitten and placing him firmly at the end of the bed, pretending that he wouldn't end up under the covers to escape the cold.

"What am I going to do with you?"

The kitten did not answer, merely stared at her as if to say, 'we both know where i'm heading'. When he inevitably crept inside the covers, his soft paws curled into a vibrating ball next to her chest, she felt that she could maybe manage the gig, as long as nothing else got in her way.

"It's alright, buddy. I won't tell if you won't."

Esther slipped into a comfortable sleep not long after, the kitten curled up beside her.

The next afternoon was overcast, and she'd been waiting outside the apartment for nearly twenty minutes, when her neighbour, Mr Bauer, came out in his dressing gown and asked if she was alright. Esther nodded, pulling her coat around her in the chill winter air.

The old man bent down to check the letterbox and then leant an arm over the fence. "And how's the demon fluff ball?"

She gasped in mock outrage. "Louis is wonderful. He can't help it if the big, scary Christmas tree is intruding into his home."

He whistled a low whistle. "That cat wasn't meant to be anyone's pet. Wild, he is."

She waved at him, as she saw Ashton pull up in his brown Ford.

"First of many, eh?" Ashton said, taking her things and putting them in the back seat, then he looked at her dress. "Looking good!"

She smoothed her purple dress, with notes on the

bodice, that Aria had made for her. "Let's just get this one done first."

"You're like the theory godmother," he said.

"I like that," she replied, with a laugh.

Esther didn't like feeling nervous about her music. Singing was her happy place, ever since she was five years old and got her very own cassette player. She used to fall asleep listening to music every night; everything from the Spice Girls to The Beatles. At school, she joined the choir. Then she moved on to solo singing lessons and music lessons.

For the last couple of years in Ledstow, it had always been Ashton and her; jamming, laughing, harmonising together. Anything could happen in the rest of her life, but music kept her grounded.

"I hope we're not late," she said, again. It wasn't the singing that set her bones vibrating and her stomach turning to jelly, if she was truly honest with herself. It was not knowing what the audience would think of her.

"Nah, we've got plenty of time," he said, waving his hand. "It's not like they have paid for tickets, anyway." He grinned across at her. "So, where is the place we're going?"

"I think it's just out of town to the South. Left here."

"Rochelle asked if I'd work on Christmas Eve," she said, "but I told her I couldn't."

"Well, you can't. You've got three jobs. And you're

leaving then for your parents' place, aren't you? Something has got to give, mate."

"I know." Esther looked out the window, as they came out of the shade of the hill. It was like a different town out here; flat, open and full of light, with new housing developments stretching almost to the lake's edge. "Are you even nervous?"

"A bit." He grinned at her. "Mostly pumped."

She tried to stop herself going over and over the lyrics to their starting song. She knew this. She could do it. "Which name are we using? Soulful?"

Ashton shrugged. "Yeah, it'll do. It's not the name that matters, it's the jams."

CHAPTER 2

It was only five minutes until they pulled up to Zany Grey's Home for the Aged. It looked like an old manor house with a low extension built on the side. Lakshmi, who was married to the brother of Esther's friend, Aria, came out to meet them, wiping her hands.

"The residents are all very excited," she said, smoothing her blue uniform. "They've had their afternoon nip, and they may be a little rowdy, I'm afraid." She mimed taking a sip from a shot glass.

"Thank you so much for this." Esther looked at all the bedrooms they passed. She wondered if Zany was in there somewhere or if it was just a made-up name. They came out of the corridor into a large lounge with green and brown armchairs all around the edge.

"Hello, dear," one of the old women said, loudly. Esther smiled at the woman, who was leaning forward on her chair, and had gold rings on her fingers.

"That's Iris. She's the self-appointed leader of the residents." Lakshmi grinned. "An absolute love, but keeps us in line." Iris made a shooing gesture, and she laughed. "You can set up here."

"Thanks," Ashton said. "We thought we'd play a few of our most popular covers, like hits from the Beatles, Cat Stevens and Neil Young."

Lakshmi raised her eyebrows. "They were really looking forward to some Christmas songs."

"Oh," Esther said. She got out her ukelele and plucked experimentally at the strings. "We can definitely fit one or two of those in."

"Is that a violin, love?" Iris said, loudly.

"It's a ukelele," she replied. Iris nodded, but didn't look entirely convinced.

Ashton leafed through their music folder.

Her phone started ringing in the bag at her feet. Seeing it was her mum, Esther made a face and swiped the red phone to dismiss the call, a twinge of guilt spiking the top of her spine. She hadn't talked to her mum since her birthday in November.

"Are you going out anywhere special tonight?" Paula asked. Esther could imagine her folding sheets while she was on the phone. She always seemed to be doing two things at once.

"Aria, Sam and Ash are coming over to the flat and we're getting some filthy takeaways and drinking wine and then we'll go out for brunch tomorrow."

"Don't you want to go out dancing?" Her mum asked. Esther almost felt hands on her back, pressing, moulding her into a shape her family liked, and could understand. "I loved dancing when I was young."

Esther knew what she was asking. "Nope. Not really." Clubs made her nauseous. Although she loved the music, it was the drunk people that she didn't like.

"And did you get my package?"

"Yeah, it was great, thanks."

"Any special men in your life at the moment?"

She sighed. "You've met Ashton, haven't you?"

"He's lovely," Paula responded. "Are you and him... ?"

"Mum, no! He's a good friend. He has a partner, anyway. Will and he have been together for years."

"Oh," she said, voice pitched high with surprise. "Well, as long as you're happy," her mother said, but it somehow seemed that it was more about what made her happy. "How's the job search going?"

"Leave her be," she heard her dad say in the background.

Esther sighed. "I've got a job. I'm working at the music store."

"Selling electric guitars to men having midlife crises, you mean?"

"Well, yeah," she admitted. "There is a bit of that. But Greg *says that I can move into a store manager role, when I get a bit more experience."*

Her mother sighed. "You're basically doing that already. We paid for a violin teacher for you for years. Why don't you teach?"

"I'm fine where I am." It was true that she'd probably earn more if she taught music. But she didn't particularly want to have to deal with young kids who didn't know what instrument they liked, and their parents, who thought they should be maestros after a few months. None of it really appealed to her.

"Oh well, just don't let your life run out before you've lived it."

"I'm living my life." What was the big rush? Why did she need everything to happen so fast? Just because her mother was married and they bought their first house at 21. She had her first child at 23 and became a judge at 28. That was a lot. By those standards, she was already a wrinkled old maid. Esther wasn't in that much of a rush. She guessed that was why she'd always been called a dreamer.

"Hello everyone, we are Soulful," Ashton said into the microphone now, his easy grin and confidence reflected in the crowd. "I think you'll maybe know this one?"

Esther dragged herself back from thoughts of her family. They started to play Yellow Submarine, an upbeat piece that their friends always enjoyed when they came to watch them practice. The people in the room immediately relaxed, some patting their knees or clapping hands gently. One man stared out the window, a beatific smile on his face.

"Deck the Halls?" Ashton whispered to her soon, when she was taking a sip from her water bottle.

She nodded. "We should just sing it, maybe. Unless you want to fudge the chords?"

"Yeah." He put his guitar to one side. Some of the residents sang along.

They started on Moon River, then played Heart of Gold. As Esther sang and played, the tension melted away from her shoulders and her voice grew stronger. She focused on Ashton's rich tenor and leaned in and the room melted away, until it was just them and the melody.

Just before the end of the song, Esther opened her eyes, to see Iris' pale face in the front row, eyes closed, head back against the chair. Another man's head dropped forward.

Alarmed, she kept watching. Iris woke up, and shook herself a little, blinking as she looked around, and Esther couldn't help but sigh in relief.

"Are you two a married couple?" It was Iris again.

"No, we're not," Ashton said, wiggling his ring-free fingers at her. "Are you offering?"

"Oh, you cheeky—"

Lakshmi came over when they were packing up and walked them out to the front desk. She had a huge grin on her face.

"The residents absolutely loved that. Now, payment-wise, I've got your bank details, haven't I? I'll have to see if we can get you back again sometime."

"Oh, yeah, definitely," Ashton said. "Our schedules are wide open."

Esther smiled at her. "Thank you so much for the opportunity."

"I think that went pretty well." Ashton walked ahead of her down the path to the car, and unlocked the passenger door for her.

"Didn't you notice that half of them drifted off to sleep?" Esther hissed.

"That's alright. They still enjoyed it," he said. "They are allowed to be tired. Most of them have probably had long, beautiful lives."

But it seemed a little odd to Esther. Christmas carols weren't exactly slow and boring. And how did they drift off to sleep while they were singing along?

Ashton got into the driver's seat, and pulled out of the carpark. "Do you want to get gelato?"

"I won't," she said. "Can we pop around the corner and see my nan? Is that alright? I'll only be fifteen minutes."

"Okay, I'll wait outside for you. I'm going to check in with my partner. He's dying to know how it went. Sent me about twelve messages."

People called this part of town 'Grey Way', because of the ages of most of the people who lived there. As she walked up the path, Esther reflected how different this rest home was to the previous one. Where Zany's was wooden, converted from a house, and set back from the road behind a row of trees, this was a large, cream box, with huge windows and a good view of passersby.

Her grandmother, Hope Daphne Forte, was looking as small as usual in her rocking chair, but her eyes brightened when she saw Esther.

"Hello, Blue Eyes," she said. The nickname had somehow stuck around from when Esther sang Sinatra at her school assembly, her high voice spinning thinly over the kids' heads in the hall. As nicknames did, it made her cringe on the inside and feel simultaneously comforted. *Like families*, she thought.

"Hi nan," she said, giving her a cuddle and inhaling her rosewater perfume. "Had your hair done?"

"Oh, yes." Hope patted her curls.

"Did you hear about that local psychic?"

"You got in before me," her grandmother said, with a twinkle in her eye. "Pretty amazing that she found the exact spot where the family ring was buried. Seems like there are more and more of these happenings nearby." She sat back and stared hard at Esther. "I've been waiting for some good conversation. Mary across the hall just wants to play checkers every day. Now, I like checkers as much as the next person, but you can have too much of a good thing, darling."

"That's fair enough," Esther said.

"And Kevin is always bossing me around. Just because he's six years younger than me. I'm not one to moan, but I'm looking forward to getting out of here at Christmastime."

"Yeah," Esther said, going around behind the chair to pull out the blanket and drape it over her grandmother's knees. "It's a bit cooler in here today."

"Oh, don't fuss," her grandmother said.

If Esther was honest, she wasn't looking forward to five days in Paunceworthy at her parents' house. It wouldn't just be her parents' questions she'd have to deal with, but her three brothers would be there as well. When was she going to get a proper job? How much money was she earning? Did she have anyone special on the scene?

Perhaps she should try that 'fake boyfriend' thing people always did in rom com movies. Who could she take along? On second thoughts, her mum would see right through that.

"They love us, really." Her grandmother's voice cut through her daydreams, with that uncanny ability to know what she was thinking about. "Did you bring me any of my books?"

"Of course." Esther reached into her bag and pulled out a book of logic puzzles and one of sudoku puzzles. "And I thought you might like some shortbread. Not homemade, sorry. But Nan, guess what we just did?"

"I couldn't possibly."

Esther sat down on the other armchair. "Only our very first gig. Ashton and I performed around the corner at another rest home."

Hope clapped her hands together. "Did you really? That's… wonderful. Tell me, how did it go?"

"Alright, I think. Some of the residents went to sleep, though."

"Oh dear," she said, undoing the wrapping on the biscuit tin, "and how did you feel while playing?"

"I loved it." Esther took two pieces of shortbread.

"Excellent. Well, you must do the same thing here, of course," she said, briskly. "I'm going to ask Brenda about it when she comes in to see me. She'll agree. She says I'm her favourite resident."

"Of course you are. Right, I've gotta go, Nan. Ashton's waiting out there. I will be back next week, though, and we might go for a stroll outside." She kissed her nan's cheek.

"Alright, love. And tell Ash 'well done'."

When she got out to the car, Ashton looked at her and grinned. "How was Hope?"

"Sharp as a tack." She shook her head, and Ashton laughed. "She sends her love, too."

He nodded. "I hope your flat's clean."

She looked sideways at him. He was grinning like the cat that got the cream.

"Relatively," she said. "Why?"

"We just did our first performance! If we want to be a real band, we have to act like it. Message the girls to come over. We're making cocktails tonight."

CHAPTER 3

$\mathcal{E}$sther's phone whirred to life, as if possessed. The chromatic scale in The Flight of the Bumblebee crashed into her morning with a hectic urgency she didn't want or need, sending an ache throbbing through her head. She fumbled for the phone before it buzzed angrily off the edge of the bedside table, and frowned at the screen.

She didn't normally answer a Private Number, and this time of day meant it would most likely be international — or her mother. That would be just her luck.

"Hello," she mumbled, voice thick with sleep, finger hovering over the 'End Call' button, ready to press it if needed.

"Esther Maria Forte?" It was a woman's voice, brisk

and businesslike. Esther sat up and brushed her hair out of her face. The sudden movement made her head swim.

"Yes?"

"I'm Detective Shona Norman." It took Esther a moment to process what the woman was saying. She hadn't had her coffee yet, and her mind was still frolicking happily in her dreams, where a certain male singer had just asked her onstage to help him with the chorus.

Detective?

"Sorry for the early phone call," she said. "We're ringing staff from Book Ends bookshop. Would that be you?"

"Ah… sort of. I don't really work at the bookshop. I go there sometimes to organise the music book stock."

The police detective barrelled on. "Rochelle didn't go home on Friday and her husband rang us, quite distressed. We're calling around the other staff who were at the bookshop to see if they might have any idea where she could be."

"What?"

"Ashton Bramwell told us that you were there and left at the same time as Rochelle. Do you know anything about where she might be? Did she mention anything to you at all?"

"No, I… " It was taking a while for the words to sink in, but as she started to understand, her pulse sped up and the nauseous feeling came back to her.

A tiny mewing came from somewhere near the floor. By the light filtering through the gap in the curtains, it was about 6am on Sunday morning and vague memories of last night's gin-fuelled Mamma Mia sing-along flashed through her mind.

She hoped her friends got home alright on the bus. Ashton and his partner left first, so they wouldn't be in quite the state she was. She felt like something the cat had coughed up. 'Never drinking again' was the phrase that came into her mind.

And what about Rochelle? Esther had been working at the bookshop with her on Friday. It was a hectic shift, that was for sure. It always was in the weeks leading up to Christmas. But otherwise, everything had been normal.

Last week, when someone selling Christmas hamper subscriptions had gotten a little too pushy in the shop, Rochelle had forcibly removed her. Jehovah's Witnesses, self-published authors with their books in hand and girl guides all got the same treatment when they knocked at the shop door. If anyone could look after herself, Esther was sure it would be Rochelle.

"Yes?" The policewoman prompted her, and Esther came back to the conversation with a jolt.

"Rochelle didn't get home on Friday night? And you're just checking up on her now?"

Esther reached over the side of the bed, where her

kitten was clawing its way up the covers from the ground. She lifted it up and placed it onto the duvet, and it curled up into a vibrating silver ball, no doubt planning its next mischief.

"Well, we have certain processes… We would prefer to discuss it in person, rather than over the phone. I know this might be distressing for you, but I need you to come down to the station for a chat."

Did she have to go in today when she felt the slightest movement would send her running to the bathroom?

"Oh, of course. Yes." Esther's palms came out in a sweat. Was this the part where they took her into custody? Forced her into a confession?

Her mind was already reeling back to when she'd first moved in here. She was next door at Mr Bauer's place when the police knocked on the door. He had bought himself a car, and the police insisted he had stolen it. It turned out he had paid cash for it, and the person who sold it owed money against it. They'd taken the cash and stopped paying the loan.

She had helped him sort it out, but the way that police officer hadn't listened to him, presumably because of his age, had chilled her.

She took a deep breath. This is just a routine chat, she told herself. Don't act guilty. Don't be nervous.

"Are you there? I'll meet you at nine. Just ask for Detective Norman."

CHAPTER 4

$\mathcal{E}$sther stopped to pick up a few dishes on the floor, stacking them together. After a quick shower, she had thrown on jeans and a sweatshirt with 'What happens at band camp' written on the front. Now it was time to clean up.

She grimaced as her hand went into the sticky chocolate sauce at the edge of the plate. They had decided to make ice cream smoothies, and, if she remembered right, sponge cake had been crumbled up and thrown in, with lashings of raspberry and chocolate sauce and chocolate chips, as well as some extras. It was all a bit fuzzy.

"What do we think?" Aria had asked, holding up a bottle of gin. The celebration had changed to planning for Aria's engagement, but was rapidly turning from party planning to cocktail planning.

"It'll be just like mum's trifle," Sam said.

Ashton just looked at them. He was drinking coffee from a large mug, and Esther wondered how he did that. At this time? She'd be awake half the night. Perhaps he was part vampire.

"Perfect." Aria had tipped the bottle over, holding it at the bottom like a bartender. "Now what music do we want at the engagement party? Esther? You can choose."

Ashton waved his hand. "Hello. Available. Good-looking."

Aria threw a cushion at him and it hit him in the side of the face.

Esther smiled, thinking of her friends. She took the plates into the kitchen and scrubbed at the sticky mess with dishwashing liquid, the lime smell rising up around her. She hummed Cell Block Tango from Chicago under her breath, sliding along to the drying rack and back to the sink.

She popped a ginger pill for the nausea, as well as her usual medicines. She looked around the lounge, checking if they had made much of a mess last night.

A coffee pouch was sitting on the low table. Esther had started getting her groceries delivered a few months ago, which was a relief when she was stuck inside with bad allergies or for that delightful week when endometriosis ruled her life each month. But when something wasn't in stock, the store often substituted with something else. This week, she had been disgusted to see they had substituted coffee for decaffeinated. Aria drank decaf, so Esther would have to drop it over to her.

The old retro bookshelves she had requisitioned from her parents looked so cool, even if she only had one shelf of books, a plant and a couple of old records in it. Straightening the couch cover and the fluffy throw that hung over the back, she nodded.

She checked over her appearance in the oval mirror, tying her brown hair into a low ponytail. Her brows could do with a pluck. She added a little lip gloss, but she still looked more 'day after' than 'ready to glow'.

The flat was quiet. A faint scrabbling noise came from somewhere near the ceiling, which she thought must be mice. Stupid old building.

"Why can't you get the mousies?" she said to Louis. "That's your job, you know." He stretched up against the wall, steadfastly ignoring her.

She opened a tin of cat food, spooned some into the bowl, and left the bowl by the kitchen door.

"Stay out of trouble," she said, firmly, in what was possibly the most redundant phrase she had ever spoken.

Esther stopped at the coffee shop around the corner from the police station. Grounds for Divorce was a trendy little place, with hanging plants trailing their tendrils down, and repurposed mismatched wooden chairs around retro tables.

She went up to the counter and perused their selection of baked goods. "A medium latté, please. And I'll have that vegetarian muffin, or, um, no… maybe the cheese scone…"

"You're in early on a Sunday morning." The barista leaned over and gave her a smile, her long ash-coloured plait swinging as she moved. Lottie had bought the coffee shop after separating from her husband last year. She knew most of her customers and their coffee orders by sight. "That's not like you."

She heard a sigh from behind her. As if chatting to a friend was outlawed now.

"Yeah, better make that a large coffee please, the larger the better," she said. She sensed the person behind her shuffling slightly, as if to indicate she was taking too long. When did people get so impatient?

"Let me get that for you now, sweetie. Hard night?"

"You could say that," she said.

Lottie winked at her. She smiled a thanks, turned around with her coffee and smacked straight into someone. Coffee splashed up in an arc from the sip hole. The biscotti fell to the floor between them with a plop.

"Ah." The policeman was about a foot taller than her. He had dark hair with a wavy bit at the front and a jawline so sharp it shouldn't be allowed. He started rubbing at the coffee spots on his shirt with his sleeve.

"Oh my gosh, I'm so sorry." Esther put her coffee down on the bench and snatched up some serviettes and passed them across. "Water, you need cold water."

"Thanks," he said, taking a serviette from her. She knelt down and wiped up a spot of liquid from the ground, feeling his eyes burn into her. Or was it her that needed cold water splashed on her face?

When Esther stood up, he left the line and headed for the bathrooms. She made her way to a table, cringing on the inside.

"Excuse me," the barista said, holding up a phone. "Did you forget this?"

Esther went back to have a look, and shook her head. "No, it's not mine. But I can give it back to him." *Because I'm a glutton for punishment,* she thought.

She went through the wooden door in the back that the policeman had disappeared through and waited in the tiled corridor until he came out of the bathroom. His shirt had dark wet splotches on it now, but it looked like the coffee marks had come off.

"Here," she said. "And I am honestly really sorry."

"Oh, thanks. It's alright, I've got some clothes at work. You seem a bit nervous," he said, then looked embarrassed, as if he'd said the quiet part out loud.

"Yeah, just a bit worried about being late." Esther

always arrived early. She guessed it stemmed from being told she was slow or lazy. So now she overcompensated by being the first one there. His stare was disquieting, but Esther felt that she was doing the same right back at him. That hint of dark stubble around that jawline.

He broke off first and looked down at the phone, and gave it a quick rub with his sleeve. "I'm running late." He held the door open.

"Sorry again," she said as she went through the door.

Looking at her watch, she had fifteen minutes. Shame still burned her cheeks every time she thought about it. It would be better to wait outside in the cool air than in a horrible waiting room.

Esther stopped on the bridge, looking into the old mill pond, which was covered in weeds. It was one of the prettiest spots in town even in the grey winter, where tourists often stopped to take a photo on their way to the hilltop trails.

When she had first arrived, she booked in for all sorts of walking tours. She wanted to know all the secrets of the quaint streets and narrow buildings. Stories passed down through time held a certain magic, even when told by bored young tour guides.

Esther knew that past the mill was the old weir that

kept the water level high. The stone walls surrounding the pond were built in the 18th century, they said, to keep the cattle out of the pond. Beyond that was the cutest little picnic spot under the willows. You could only get there by climbing onto the old walls and walking around the narrow bank.

A siren came from the lower town somewhere, and some children yelled down at the playground. Her favourite story about the town was that Ledstow used to be surrounded by stone walls which made it a formidable and easily defendable spot, and there were rumours that the ghosts of the soldiers that guarded the walls still walked their beat. She had told her grandmother that one.

Watching the sparrows on the grass, Esther wondered how it would go with the police. She knew that being the last one to see Rochelle after work looked bad.

That same rasping whisper that she had heard near her house was coming from nearby. A blue bird hopped along the branch opposite her and jumped down, landing neatly on the end of a broken-off twig. It bobbed its head up and down, almost as if it was nodding. It had white along the edges of its wings and the tips of its tail and a white body. A magpie flew across to one of the telegraph poles.

Were there usually this many birds? Had the Environment Group done some re-wilding around here? She would likely have heard about it from Jo. The blueish grey bird glided down and landed on the grass and the sparrows scattered, some landing on the oak, some flying up to the roof of the millhouse. One perched on the road sign. Was the blue one just slightly bigger than the others, so they knew to be wary?

It eyed her with a slightly too knowing look, cocking its head from side to side. It lifted its wings up as if greeting the other birds. She shook herself off. Knowing look?

Just get this over with first, she told herself. She sipped her coffee, and let the warmth of the cup soothe her. *Afterwards, I can lose it and escape into a blanket fort with some books.*

A carful of tourists, with bikes on the roof rack, headed into the gorge. Esther watched them pass, envious of their freedom. The wind in their faces. Esther would always remember the first time she rode a bike.

She must have been about nine, since her hair was almost down to her waist. Her brothers were probably playing cricket and she was playing at a house down their street.

She had tried to ride her bike a few times before, and Violette thought it was really funny to see her wobble along. She brought it over with her most days, hoping that one day it would just click.

That day, they had moved on to skipping, and Violette

asked her little brother, Stefan, to hold one end, while she held the other.

Esther jumped the rope without a problem, and went around to take the end of the rope.

"Two little sausages," she said.

A car pulled slowly into the driveway, and they moved onto the lawn. "Get out of the way when there's a car," their father said, his red face emerging from the window.

"Two little sausages, sizzling in a pan," Esther chanted, still standing on the edge of the concrete. "One went pop..."

When she got to bang, Mr Hunter exploded.

A tiny part of her brain zapped her body into action, and her legs were moving before she knew it. She ran down the driveway and back towards home along the endless blurry road.

When she finally got to her driveway, she saw a familiar figure, wearing a long blue dress and colourful scarf. Esther ran straight into her arms.

"Nan!"

"Blue Eyes," she said, hugging her tight, stumbling back a bit at the force of the collision.

Esther pulled back, to look at her nan's beautiful blue necklace and paisley scarf. She picked the necklace up, feeling the cool weight of it.

"Why did you come over?"

"I just thought I might be needed today," her nan said, with a sort of half smile. "Mercury is in retrograde. Come on, let's go inside."

Esther was about to ask what she meant, when she stepped back, and glanced down the road. "I... forgot my bike."

"Can you pop back and get it, sweetie?"

Esther shook her head. Mr Hunter was now impossibly tall to her, and she felt one word from his mouth would send children scattering away, like when she dropped a leaf onto the line of ants in her garden.

"I'll come with you."

She walked down the road towards the Hunters' place, and waited outside, while her nan grabbed the bike and walked it out.

She set it firmly in front of Esther on the narrow street, pointing towards home.

"Come on," she said. "I've got all the time in the world."

Esther got on. She imagined a wristwatch that contained a whole planet, slowly revolving, and quite liked that idea. All the time in the world. She knew she wouldn't be able to ride the bike, but she could humour her nan, who would probably just laugh and pick her up once she tipped over. She put her foot on the pedal and pushed down.

Her nan walked ahead of her and started to clap her hands.

"You can... do it... Esther..." she chanted. Everything inside her was telling her not to do it, that she would have a terrible accident. A dog barked somewhere.

Esther's foot slipped off the pedal, and she put it down. Her *hands on the handlebars were slippery so she wiped them on her pink tights. The footpath looked all smudged through the tears, hot behind her eyes. She blinked them away.*

She gave it another go, pushing along with her sandaled foot.

"You can..." Her grandmother's voice was as sweet to her ears as a lullaby and a warmth spread through her. "Do it..."

Esther found herself flying along on the bike, hands gripping the handlebars tight. She wasn't even sure how she did it in the end, but she was bumping along. Her legs were going around and the air was cool in her face, until she came up to her house and realized she didn't know how to stop.

She looked at her nan who was smiling, and the bike kept going — straight into a bush.

When she stood up, her knee stung, and her arms were scratched.

Wiping snot and tears from her face, she stood up and smiled. "I did it," she said.

She breathed deeply now, holding onto the cold rail of the bridge. When her anxiety got too much, she sometimes imagined herself running far away through the woods, and building a little house in a clearing by a brook. Just to breathe.

But when she thought about the place she wanted to end up, the image in her mind's eye somehow ended up as Ledstow, with its mismatched buildings and narrow streets, the river snaking its way beneath bridges and over weirs and the gorge slicing through the hills behind.

She loved popping into the coffee shop and chatting to Lottie, sitting in the sun with a book. She loved browsing the market in the town square with Aria. Picnics at the reserve. Afternoons at the lake or curled up in the library. Ledstow felt like home.

"Hi, I'm Shona Norman. " The policewoman walked towards her with her hand out. Robust was the first word that went through Esther's mind. The woman had short, sandy hair streaked through with greys, and purple glasses. Her lips pressed together in a hard line and her eyes flicked to the clock on the wall. "Esther? I talked to you earlier."

"Good morning."

"Come with me." The woman walked down a hallway, stepping to the side to let someone pass. It was the officer from the coffee shop, now wearing a jersey over his, no doubt damp, shirt.

"I'll take this one," the man said, looking hard at her. Esther wanted to sink into the floor. He and Shona walked over to the side and discussed, with lots of hand gestures, for a minute, then she came back. Esther wished they would hurry up. She wanted to get it over with, get back to her Sunday morning, lying on the couch in front of some trashy tv shows, with Rochelle safe at home.

"This is Clark. Do you mind if he joins us?"

"We've met," he put in.

Esther sighed, thinking what fun it would be to be publicly shamed twice, by the same person, in one day. "That's fine."

She followed Shona into a small meeting room. Clark pulled out two chairs and sat down in one.

Shona stood. "So, can you tell us everything that happened that day, Friday. Whether you think it's relevant or not, please?"

"I went into Book Ends on Friday at about two. I work there for a few hours at a time, only when I'm merchandising the music books, you know, putting new stock in, if any have been sold. Organising them, making them look pretty."

They questioned her at length about that shift at the bookshop. "It was hectic," she said, for the fiftieth time. "So busy. I was just in my little corner for most of it."

"And what happened after you left the shop?"

"I walked down the alleyway with her."

"Did anything strange happen?" Shona pressed.

"No, I don't think so. A light was out in the alleyway —" She stopped.

"Okay." Shona turned to Clark, who wrote something

down. "Did she seem distressed at all? Give any indication that she was leaving?"

"She was stressed out, as any retail store owner would be at this time of year."

"And then?"

"I almost got hit by someone on a bike," she said. Clark frowned.

There was a pause. "Okay, if you only work at the bookshop once a fortnight, how come you were there on Thursday and Friday last week?"

She looked up. Shona's eyes were hard and calculating.

"How did you—?"

"We asked for the timesheets," Clark put in, almost apologetically.

"Right. Well, I wasn't keeping any secrets," she said, taken aback that they were testing her honesty like that. But why should she be surprised? That was their job. "Sometimes I'm asked to go in and help when they have a lot of stock to put on display. Like around major holidays."

Shona was quiet for a moment, then let out a sigh. "Our problem is that, with everything we've pieced together, you were the last person to see Rochelle. Please make absolutely sure you've given us all the information that you possibly can. We want to find her as quickly as possible."

Esther fiddled with her leather handbag strap on her lap. Her palms were sweating. The two police officers were being perfectly polite, but she was beginning to feel like she was tied to the railway tracks with a very large train heading towards her.

Her heart sped up, as their eyes burned into her. "I wasn't the last, though," she blurted. "There was someone else there that night."

"Who?"

She remembered the grizzled cheeks, two faded jackets to protect against the cold footpath, the grateful look on his face, the woollen hat with the startling blue eyes beneath.

"I don't know his name, but maybe I could draw him."

"Excuse me for a moment," Detective Norman said, looking at her mobile phone. She stood up and went to talk in the corridor.

Esther took the paper and pencil that Clark gave her and brushed her fingers through her hair. Her scalp was prickling with sweat.

"Are you alright?" Clark asked her, a slight frown creasing his brow. "Do you want some water?" He went over to the water filter and poured her a cup.

"It feels like getting grilled by my parents," she said, sketching out a quick outline and fiddling with her pencil while she recalled the details around his eyes, brows and mouth.

"We're a couple of local police officers in a small town," he said. "It's hardly NYPD." Close up, she could see he had hazel eyes, and his brows were lowered in a concerned frown.

"Generalised anxiety disorder, yay. It makes me jump right to the worst-case scenario in my head." She sat back and took a drink of the freezing cold water. Then she shaded in the thick eyebrows, cleft chin.

"Right," he said, nodding. "That is one great picture," he added, leaning over her shoulder to look. "I even think I might know who you mean. You're really talented. I'm sorry about saying you seemed dodgy before. Of course, your friend is missing."

"Thanks," Esther said quietly. "She isn't really a friend."

Clark looked sharply at her.

Detective Norman poked her head back into the room, smoothing her hair back off her face. "Clark, can I have a word for a minute?"

He went out, and pulled the door to behind him. Esther put her ear to the crack, her pulse racing. She couldn't stop thinking about the light being out in the alleyway. Was it something sinister?

"We've just found a body that matches Rochelle's description," she said. "We will need to contact the next of kin to identify the body."

"Damn. I think we can let Esther go, then."

Esther looked down and saw that drops of cold water had spilled onto her hand. She couldn't even feel it as her whole body seemed to have gone numb. Absurdly, she wanted to giggle. Should a policeman be saying 'damn'?

She heard the glug of the water filter and the ticking of the clock on the wall.

"Oh, of course. Yes."

Shona's clipped tones were back to business, as they came back in. "We'll be in touch if we need to speak with you again."

"I'll take her back out the front." Clark took the cup off her and placed it on the bench, then gently helped her stand up.

At the front door, he said, "Is there anything I can do to help? You'll all be offered counselling, of course."

"Okay," she said. "Thanks. I'll call my friend." She looked down on her phone from what felt like a great distance and jabbed at the screen.

When Aria heard her voice, she said, "I'll be right there."

Esther sat in one of the chairs in the waiting area, looking straight ahead. The policeman sat down, with one seat between them.

"How's the shirt?" she asked, after a while.

"Soggy," he said, and she laughed.

"You don't have to wait with me, you know."

"I know. But I'm not going anywhere."

CHAPTER 5

"It's a bit exciting, isn't it?" asked Aria. Her eyes twinkled, and she grabbed an apple out of the bowl and took a bite.

"Aria!" Her friend had taken the morning off work, met her at the police station and walked her home. It was only after many cups of hot chocolate and a huge slice of cake that she felt her body was able to move again.

Her friend tucked one of her dark braids into the bun on top of her head. "What do you think happened to her? Heart attack?"

She gave Aria an exasperated look. "I wish I knew."

"Well, nothing much happens here, otherwise. And I'm basically an old woman, now that I'm engaged. Don't married women have an obligation to gossip?"

"I don't know about that," she said. "It sounds like you

got that from a Jane Austen novel. Are you having second thoughts about getting married at all?"

"He called me Arrietty the other day," she said, flatly.

Esther stifled a laugh. "Well, that is your name."

"Only my dad calls me that. And only if I deserve it." She shrugged, and let her shoulders droop down. "I'm not actually sure what's wrong, I've just got a feeling that something is coming. I'm really not sure if we know each other well enough."

"Are you just worried, though? You've been busy at work since your colleague left."

"Could be."

Esther thought she didn't sound convinced, and got up to look in the kitchen for a sweet salve for the soul. "I must have something better than an apple to eat," she called.

At times like this, her nan would normally bake scones. Esther picked the recipe folder out of the shelf, ran her hand over the pages that were spotted with grease and dog-eared by time, and turned to the recipe, 'Hope's Best Scones for a Rainy Day'. She turned the oven on and pulled out a tray.

Esther was still thinking about the trip home coming up.

The family home loomed up in her mind's eye, a country house that was way too large for her parents and one brother who still lived there. The gardens were always impeccable and the lawn made you scared to put a toe on it. One of the upstairs rooms was beautifully furnished and occasionally used for paying guests now, but it used to be the room her two older brothers shared.

She would have been five years old when the first odd thing had happened. It wasn't long since the mysterious symbols on buildings had become words like 'sale' and 'stop', and young Esther had looked out of the back seat in the car, wide-eyed, at a world that suddenly had meaning.

On this night, her dream had frightened her, and the carpet was cool where her bare foot touched it, as if this silvery shadowed room was quite a different one from her own. She jumped away from the bed and padded along the hall, careful not to look back. She thought she had been asleep for hours, but lights were on downstairs so she headed for the landing. Flickering shadows like the creatures in her dream followed alongside, as she trotted past the room that Brad and Phillip shared, and Aaron's room, where loud snores could be heard.

"This is the last time," she heard, and her mother's voice was raised. Esther stopped, one hand on the bannister. It sounded like her mother was talking to a kid, but she couldn't hear any of her brothers banging around.

"Esther's fast asleep."

She crouched down and pressed her face to the wooden bars to see who was in the lounge. She thought it was her grandmother, and another woman. She desperately wanted to go down and see her nan, press her face into her silky scarf and touch the blue locket around her neck.

"Of course I checked," her mum said, after a pause.

Esther wiggled her feet. They were starting to go numb with cold.

She stretched up to look at the barometer, and its fancy curlicued needle pointed to, 'Change'. She was never sure what was going to change. Was it her? But she remembered now — one of her brothers had said, "It means it's going to rain, dummy."

She had so many questions. Her family didn't give her the answers she wanted. Usually, they said she would know what they were talking about when she was older. Esther made up her stories to fill this gap, on the school bus, or when it was her turn to do the dishes, hands soaped up, staring out the window at the top of the oak tree.

She dreamed up a tale that her parents had desperately wanted a fourth child. When they saw Esther, they knew instantly she was the perfect fit for their family, bringing kindness and creativity to the family of analytical and hardworking people. This story gave her a warm feeling around her breastbone.

Esther bumped the barometer and it swung against the wall, setting her heart racing. She shrunk back around the corner as someone came to the bottom of the stairs, then came out and sat on that second top step again. It felt important that she see what was happening.

"Come on Matty," a woman's voice said. "There's nothing there." Esther thought it sounded like the lady from the grocer's shop. Perhaps her mum was having one of those Tupperware parties.

"Are you sure?"

"It's getting worse."

"Alright, I'm ready." Her mum sighed, and stood up. She had a wine glass in her hand. Another woman, with a tear-streaked face, nestled in close. Esther recognized the coloured cardigan. It was Mrs Hurst, who once gave her an apple free of charge. Matilda, she remembered. Her mother put her arm around Matty's shoulders and swayed side to side, in and out of Esther's view.

Her mum hummed a song, quiet at first but getting louder. Mrs Hurst had a beatific smile on her face. As they moved, the wine in her mother's glass sloshed around, but no one seemed to notice.

If Esther was holding juice over that carpet, she would have been in big trouble. Adults could be weird when they were drinking wine.

"Thanks, dear," Mrs Hurst said, wiping tears from her eyes.

"You're welcome. You deserve happiness," her mother said, her voice sharp with emotion.

Esther turned away, surprised and reassured at this show of affection by her mum. She padded along the hallway back to bed, sure she would be able to get back to sleep.

She put the butter in to soften in the microwave, as

she thought back to the memories that niggled at her mind. Even at five, she had known, on some level, that the way her mum treated her was not the same as the relationship some other kids had with their mum.

But as Esther rubbed the butter into the flour, she reflected that scones were something that she knew. Scones would rise, and she'd cut them into fluffy halves and melt butter on top, and they'd taste of childhood. No matter what happened in Ledstow, or how many times she embarrassed herself, her scones would rise.

"You're baking?" her friend called out. "You must be in a bad way."

Esther shook herself out of her daydreams to notice the warming light had turned off. She slid the tray into the oven and shut the door.

Aria appeared in the kitchen doorway, with Louis tucked under one arm, and Esther winced. The kitten would hardly let her pick him up like that. "Be careful."

"Don't worry, he loves me," Aria said. She leaned on the bench, and held Louis close to her chest. "So did you see any hot men in uniform today? Oh, I suppose you weren't really looking."

Esther gave a noncommittal noise. Any nice-looking men with stubbled jawlines and kind eyes that she had seen today now thought she was a quivering, ridiculous mess.

"I can clean up, if you like. Just like old times." Aria gently set Louis down on the floor.

"That would actually be great," she said.

On Monday, Esther struggled to concentrate at work. The shop was called Guitar Pharaoh, and it was next to the bed and bath shop, which meant that bored partners often wandered in, lured in by the drum sets and shiny guitars. They were never going to buy anything.

She stood behind the desk, fiddling with the gimmicky instruments near the cash register. A box of harmonicas and ocarinas were all jumbled up, from being touched by little hands. She grabbed a cloth and gave them a polish, then decided to do a quick stocktake.

Esther had worked there for a while, and her boss, Hugh, relied on her a little too much. This morning, he stood awkwardly in front of her, and when she looked up, he said, "You know, you can have a day off if you like."

"How did you know?"

"She was my client," he said. "I got an email from her husband this morning."

She. It was interesting that people were afraid to speak the name of someone who had died.

"I know that you knew her," he said.

"Yes, but I'm fine here at work," she said, firmly.

"Okay," Hugh said, and his shoulders dropped with relief. "Great. I mean, that's fine." Duty done, he went back into his office, and the television noise started up again.

The next few days were a blur of group messages with the bookshop staff and cups of hot, sweet, tea, which she sipped behind the front desk. She leafed through trashy magazines without reading them. A woman asked her where the saxophone reeds were, and she pointed to the far wall.

Esther's phone buzzed along on the desk. She picked it up when 'Hope' appeared on the screen.

"Hello, darling."

"Hi, nan. Do you need help with the sudoku?"

"Cheeky." Her nan was the expert at sudoku puzzles, and often finished them in record time. "Of course not."

"What's going on?" she asked.

"Get your songs ready." Hope's voice was shaking with excitement. "Brenda said you can come and play for us on Friday afternoon."

"Really? But that's only two days away."

"Yes, I know. It's not a problem for you, Blue Eyes. She said there is an email on the way to you too."

"How cool! Thank you."

Just before she hung up, she added, "I told her you'd play us some nice Christmas carols."

A small part of Esther fizzed with excitement.

Another chance to sing with Ashton. But they wanted rotten Christmas carols? And just two days to prepare?

Her mind kept fixating on Rochelle. What had happened? She was also replaying the coffee shop incident and the interview with the two police people, cringing about her responses. Had she really spilt coffee on the cop that was in charge of the case? Fate really had a twisted sense of humour sometimes.

It would be fine. She probably wouldn't have to see Clark again, she told herself, flicking through the items on the desk. She had just shrugged off the embarrassment, when Hugh came in, carrying two hot drinks.

"Here's your hot chocolate. Don't spill it on the ocarinas, for God's sake."

She flushed all over again. Ugh. She had to talk to Ashton. She flicked her phone over and sent a quick text.

Lunch?

Please.

The usual. See you at 1.

Esther found it hard to make friends as an adult. Her two best friends had been around since she moved here, but everyone she met through work seemed obsessed with money, and the proper order of events in life. She preferred to listen to the rhythm of things, take things slowly. But when she got to know Ashton, she was happy to find that there were other people around like her after all.

When Ashton started at the bookshop, she had asked him about the music and films he liked. One night, he asked her along to the staff bingo night, which turned into a karaoke evening. She found out he was keen on singing, and they started their group, 'just for fun'. They were never going to perform, but their friends enjoyed their practices so much that they pushed them to do it. Then Aria arranged the gig at the rest home without even telling them.

Esther was walking down Mill Street when she saw someone who looked vaguely like that policeman. It was weird, once you had met someone new, that your brain superimposed their image on strangers' faces, she thought.

She caught the words, 'Book Ends' in the conversation as she passed, and craned her neck to look. It was, in fact, him, and she had to get closer. He was dining with an older man, seated outside at one of the tourist trap cafés in the old town. There was a little hedge planted in planter boxes, so if she crouched on the other side, he definitely wouldn't be able to see her. She leant against the wall of the locksmiths to tie her shoe.

"So we're a bit stuck now," he said. "The homeless guy was a dead end; just a waste of time. No-one else has any motive. I am thinking she probably did it herself," he said.

Esther shook her head. There was no way that

Rochelle would do that. She leaned closer to the bushes as he dropped his voice.

"The body was found in the alleyway. We haven't got the post mortem results yet. And we haven't even pinned down the time of death. There is one person..."

Just then, Esther saw her friend, Aria, crossing the road and making straight for her. She made frantic 'cut it out' movements, making a cross with her arms, but Aria had a huge smile on her face.

"Esther! Guess what!"

Two faces popped up over the hedge and Esther quickly changed her cross to an over the top, two-handed wave.

"What is it?" she said, heading off, but not before she had caught Clark's eye, her cheeks flaming hot. His face looked bemused rather than angry.

"Just some hot off the press news." Aria trotted to catch up. She was swinging her handbag and looked like the cat that had got the cream. With oversized sunglasses and a leather jacket fitted perfectly to her tall, thin, frame, Esther felt like she was walking next to a model.

Aria was the face of Hotel Ledstow, an old manor that had been turned into a 5-star hotel. She spoke three languages fluently, and was effortlessly graceful. She didn't earn a lot but was often given beautiful, expensive presents, like handbags and bracelets, by grateful guests.

Esther was dying of curiosity but decided not to beg.

"I've got some good news too," she said. "We're playing another gig at a rest home."

"Hmm. You might need to find some more contemporary songs," she said, hopping lightly over a crack in the footpath. "Because my news is that Troy and I want the highly sought-after band Soulful to play at our engagement party!"

"What!"

"It's not massive. Just sixty people, I think."

"Are you joking?" Aria shook her head. "That's our biggest audience so far. And some of them might even stay awake until the end!"

Esther had known Aria for long enough that when her friend said it would be a small gathering, she expected double the guests. Aria had a huge family with five siblings and she didn't seem to be bothered by being around a lot of people like Esther did. A real gig!

Aria nudged her affectionately with her elbow. "We're going to give you forty five minutes after the speeches."

"Oh! Ash will be pumped! I'm just off to meet him for lunch now. Join us if you like."

"Tell him hi from me. I've got to have lunch with my dad." She made a face and Esther squeezed her arm in sympathy.

"Just breathe," she said to her friend. She had been raised by her dad alone, and to say that he was protective was putting it mildly.

"He's still trying to find anything wrong with Troy that he can."

"You're his little angel."

Aria laughed bitterly. "If only he knew." She kissed Esther on the cheek and turned off down the street.

"Guess what!" She managed to hold it in until after they ordered. Then she patted the table to get Ashton's attention.

"Mm?"

"We've got not one, but two gigs coming up." She explained about the engagement party and then told him about her nan's rest home.

Ashton raised his eyebrows at her. "Two days away… we can do that. And then the party. Paid singers, baby."

"We'll just play almost the same set we played last time. We should try to fit in a practice session, though."

He nodded. "Easy."

"How are you always so calm?" she said, exasperated. While she mostly loved that side of him, a small part of her wondered what it would take to get him fired up.

He shrugged, and grinned up at the waiter as the fries arrived at the table.

"Did you know her that well?" she asked, wrapping a

chip in a serviette and blowing on it, and they both knew who she was talking about.

"I don't think I did," Ashton said, dipping a long chip in the sauce. "But how well do you truly know anyone? I've only been there for… eighteen months?"

"Mm. Yeah, because you started when Vicky left." For the first time, Esther looked back carefully on what she knew about Rochelle.

When she first turned up at the bookshop, Rochelle, a curvy woman with bold dark red lipstick and a severe bob, paused to look her over. She went back to wiping the counter down, re-arranging the pens and toys by the till. Esther had explained what she was there for, and gave a friendly smile.

Rochelle nodded. "Just don't mess up my books or scare the customers," she said, and turned away, already talking to someone else.

Esther didn't have any idea whether the woman liked her or not, so she mostly kept out of her way. It took her a year before Esther was allowed to call Rochelle anything other than Mrs Farmer. Once, she had asked Rochelle how long she had owned the bookstore, just making small talk, and Rochelle snapped back that she inherited it.

Vicky Donahue worked there too, when Esther started. She was a quiet woman, with perfectly straightened hair as if she had never slept and a long, elegant nose. She was most animated when she was talking about the latest supplement or a new yoga class she'd tried. She did all the tasks in the shop, from ordering stock to reconciling accounts to serving customers with the same detached determination. Rochelle rolled her eyes every time Vicky spoke.

"Do you think it might have been some underlying sickness that she didn't know she had?"

He shrugged. "Yeah, it could be. You sometimes hear of people ignoring symptoms until it's too late. Don't really know. Oh, did you pick up your script from the pharmacy?"

"Yeah."

"I thought she was a bit hard-nosed, to be honest," he said, quietly. "Fine as a boss. She always treated me ok, but I heard the way she talked about some of the others. She once said Vicky was stuck-up and she called Jo a workaholic."

"Outspoken, yeah."

"It makes you wonder a bit. How would people describe me if something happened? Let's remember Ashton Jeremiah Bramwell. Makes jokes at inappropriate times. Can always be found near the food table at parties."

"Sings like a freaking angel," she put in.

"Takes one to know one," he said, shoving four chips into his mouth at once.

Esther made a face at him. "So on that Friday night shift, we had Jayden, Jo, me, and you at the shop. Phoebe turned up and that weird guy Mr Deed was also around."

"Why doesn't he ever buy anything? Let's count you and me out, for a start."

"I should hope we can count out everyone else we work with as well."

He shrugged. "Look, my aunt Poppy worked with a guy who murdered his wife for a year." He caught himself and rolled his eyes. "Don't say it. He murdered his wife once. They worked together for a year before that!"

Esther snorted, in spite of herself.

"You never truly know anyone," Ashton said, and Esther looked up at him.

"I am an open book. And so are you."

"Okay, what's my favourite dinner?" he asked, a smug look on his face.

Esther put her head on the side, considering. "Something hot and spicy. I'm thinking of vindaloo. But vegan, of course. What's mine?"

"You'd like some sort of grilled chicken with lots of fresh veggies. Burritos?"

"Probably," she said. "Anyway, I think we should clear everyone that was there. It will make us feel better, at least."

"You know, that's not a bad idea," he said.

Esther tapped on the table, thinking. "Jo said they

were going out for a nice anniversary dinner with their partner. Do you remember where?"

"Shit, um, I think it might have even been in Bristol. I saw the photos on their Insta."

"Oh yeah, I think you're right," she said. "That counts them out, then. What about Jayden?"

"He's just a young chap," Ashton said, "but I can chat to him."

"Vicky wasn't there. She doesn't come into the shop much now."

"We're not bad at this," he said.

But Esther was sure things were going to get much harder.

CHAPTER 6

Esther stared at the text, as if willing the words to make sense. *I think you should come over this afternoon.* Normally, a message might start with 'hey, how are you?'. Her mind spun off in fifty directions at once.

She was busy in the music shop, but had stopped just to check her phone on her break. She'd already checked the shop emails for her boss, and paid the unpaid invoices for her boss. Then, coffee in hand, she sat on the stool by the counter, and was faced with this cryptic message from Phoebe, the lady who did the cleaning at the bookshop. They knew each other well enough, but had never been to each other's homes.

She looked around. Two customers hovered around the drumsets, now and again sitting down to have a bash. It didn't sound like they had been introduced to rhythm or beat. Esther had already been over there and offered them the digital drumsets, which were small and portable and great for beginners. The best part was that you could plug them into headphones and they didn't disturb the neighbours — or the other people in the shop. They nodded along, then went back to sitting at the full size set, twirling drumsticks.

She sighed, debating whether to say she was busy. She finally sent a quick message back. *Sure. See you about four.*

The door opened a crack and Phoebe's long-lashed blue eye appeared.

"Thank you so much for coming." She bustled Esther inside and shut the door behind her, then sat on the couch, leg jiggling.

"How are you?" Esther asked. The floor was dirty, with crumbs and the odd bit of glitter shining amongst the threads of beige. A murky fishbowl sat in the corner on a greasy-looking table. She guessed the old adage about cobblers' children having no shoes also worked for cleaners having messy houses.

"Oh! Do you want a drink?" Phoebe jumped up, and went into the kitchen. "Um, juice or tea?"

"Tea, please. What's up, Phoebe?"

She clattered around, rinsing cups without looking.

"Well, I've been thoroughly questioned by the police, but luckily, my mum was with me after that. She headed back home yesterday. I am struggling a bit. Milk?"

"No, just black, thanks. It's a lot to take in, eh?" Esther stood at the door to the kitchen, reading over the artwork on the fridge. Her eyes widened as she saw one of the pictures that was done in heavy pencil. It had what looked like four people in a coffin, and a man with a cross walking towards them. It was titled 'Our Family.'

Phoebe nodded. She saw where Esther was looking, and rubbed at her temple. "Okay, I can explain. That was mum, me and the kids having a picnic. We are not drinking blood, we are drinking orange juice. And the cross is a toy sword, okay?"

"Right. Okay," Esther said, and smothered a smile.

"Since the shop is shut, I'm... worried about how I'm going to pay the rent for the next few weeks. I've got a little bit of savings, but then, I really don't want to have to move back to my parents' house with the kids, away from friends. My mum is a midwife, so she will have plenty of opinions about how I'm raising the kids." She grimaced.

"I get that," Esther said, with feeling. "Can you ask for more hours at your other job?"

"Not really, in winter. I know that you're looking into this whole horrible thing. And I want to know what happened just as much as the next person. I really have a strong feeling there was foul play. Just maybe... don't be cross at me, but just..."

"What is it?"

"Don't count your mate out, entirely."

Esther fumbled her cup back onto the saucer. "Ashton? I absolutely know... "

"Yes," Phoebe said, barrelling on as if she knew Esther would argue. "You know how I get there after closing time? Well, one day a couple of weeks ago, I arrived a bit early, because my neighbour was looking after the kids that evening, instead of the babysitter who usually does."

Esther made a motion with her hand to keep going.

"I let myself in and heard raised voices in the shop. I said hello but they didn't hear me. It was Ashton, and he said, "How long have I worked here? This is it. I've had enough."

"And Rochelle was there as well? That doesn't sound like Ashton at all."

"I've never heard him like that. And Rochelle said 'What's the matter with you? I wanted to make you Assistant Manager, but I can't now.'"

Esther pondered this, while she sipped her hot tea. She thought there was a hint of lemon too.

"She owned this place, you know." Phoebe waved her hand around at the little sunny room.

"Yeah, I know."

"She offered it to me, when no-one else would rent me a flat. I don't have any biscuits, sorry."

"Why is that?" Esther asked. "That nobody else would rent you a place, I mean."

"I was a pregnant, single woman with a toddler. Would you take a chance on me?"

"I would," she said, lifting her cup to her lips again.

"Well, most people wouldn't. Rochelle let me stay with her for a while, but I needed my own place. I was on the waiting list for council housing and I was getting pretty desperate. And pretty fat, with the wee one in there." She patted her flat belly, and Esther found it hard to imagine her pregnant. "I thought I'd have to go back to Aberdeen, to my parents. That would not be good."

"You don't get on with your olds? Mine can be pretty challenging too." Esther sighed.

"They're very old-fashioned, shall we say? Like, they would have been fixed on finding me a man straight away."

Esther wondered how Phoebe had ended up pregnant and homeless, but thought it wouldn't be polite to ask. "How long have you been working at the shop?" she asked, instead.

"Four years, it must be," Phoebe said, walking over to the sink. She pulled a plate off the rack and dried it with a tea towel. "She was the one who pushed me to start my wee cleaning business. Gave me my first contract."

"It sounds like she really helped you out a lot."

She fiddled with the ends of the dish towel, as she looked out the window. "Yeah, I suppose she did," she said. "But I never really thought of it like that. She made everything she did seem like an accident. If I ever thanked her, she'd just say, 'Don't be stupid. You'd do the same.' I don't know if I would, though. The funny part is that I have never missed a single rent payment in two years."

Esther tried to gently bring the conversation back to Rochelle. "It sounds like you really miss her."

She shrugged slightly, and looked around. "It doesn't feel real. She's everywhere here, and at the shop."

Esther shivered. "Come on. Let's sit down."

"I know exactly what she'd say if she was here," Phoebe said, perching on the edge of the couch. "She'd tell me to sort myself out. Work harder."

"I'm not being rude, but why are you telling me about the money?" she asked Phoebe. "I'm happy to support you. But there's nothing I can do about it, really."

"I don't know." Phoebe looked down at the cuddly toy she had picked up, pulling on one leg, absently. "You're good at this stuff. I always end up telling you what's wrong, even if I don't mean to. Remember when we talked at work drinks and I was upset that my son had said he hated me? You made me feel so much better."

Esther did remember. She didn't know why, but people did tell her things.

"You don't seem to judge." Phoebe paused, then asked a question very fast so that Esther wasn't sure if she heard right. "Have you ever seen or heard anything unexplained?"

Esther whipped her head around. "What?"

But Phoebe waved her hand. "There is one more thing. I'm halfway through a publishing course, and I'm really worried that I won't be able to keep on with it. Rochelle was paying for it through work."

Esther leaned back. "Oh," she breathed. "I see."

"I know I shouldn't be thinking about it right now. But I'm really enjoying it. I'd like to start a small publisher one day."

"I mean, you can't help what you think about. I don't think there's any right way to do all this." She stood up and grabbed her bag. "I'll come with you to talk to Rochelle's husband. We'll sort it out."

"Thank you."

"Why did you ask me that before? About unexplained things?"

"Oh, don't worry. Like, I was wondering if you ever feel suffocated by your past, I guess. I can't seem to get away from my granddad. Even though he has been dead for eighteen years. He was a terrifying man."

"I'm sorry." Esther patted her on the arm, the hairs at

the top of her spine standing on end. Surely it was just Phoebe's conscience that she was hearing. Everyone had a little voice inside them, didn't they? "I think you are such a strong lady, Phoebe. You're doing well with your business, and your kids."

But she seemed to be hanging back.

"Is there anything else?"

"I had to tell them," Phoebe blurted. "About Ashton."

Friday came, and Esther tucked her music folder into her work bag.

She walked to the shop for her shift, wrapped in her warmest coat and a new scarf. A harassed looking woman bustled past her with two huge shopping bags. The jewellery shop owner was putting out his signs on the footpath, and he gave her a wave.

"Morning," she said to Mark, who worked in the cheese shop. He was a keen guitarist and often came into Guitar Pharaoh. Esther could put up with the vague odour of Roquefort that clung to him, because he had great taste in music. She had found new favourites more than once from his recommendations.

The grass in the reserve was tipped with frost. As she walked past the mill pond, she hummed a tune to herself. There were always things to look forward to; Aria's engagement party, spending the Christmas break with her family, and summer.

Something small jumped along the grass.

"Frogs!"

To her embarrassment, she realized she had said it out loud.

An old woman was looking at her from where she was feeding the ducks. "What was that, dear?"

"Nothing."

That policeman, Clark, started crossing over the bridge towards her. Her heart sank. Why did he have to be there?

"Hello," she said, cheeks heating up.

"Are you alright?" He kept looking at her with that same stare.

"Yeah, I'm fine. I just noticed something weird."

He turned his back and pointed to the trees in the distance.

"I come down here most mornings, and stop over the other side. You can see the lake's edge just there. We used to holiday down there, my mum and I. That's where I learnt to swim. Caught my first fish there."

He turned away and looked over the millpond.

"It's nice at the lake. So you grew up near here?"

"No, I just came here for the summer holidays. What did you notice? Was it the frogs?"

"Yes, it was." His chopping and changing of subjects left her a bit dizzy.

He pointed. "There's one down there that looks like it might have died. They normally hibernate in winter, so it's unusual that they've come out anyway."

"Oh, do they?" Esther had the overwhelming feeling that she had made the frogs come out of the ground herself. She felt slightly sick.

"Very strange."

To stop him from staring at her, she said, "Anyway, I was meaning to ask…"

He frowned.

"Just wondering if you had talked to the man from my picture?" she asked, before he could say anything. Like ask her about why she felt so guilty about the frogs.

"I can't really discuss—"

"Because I think he might be able to help. And I know who it isn't."

He sighed. "We've tried talking to him. Are you interfering in the investigation?"

"People just talk to me," she said. "I can't help it."

He leaned his back against the railings, and his eyes flicked back to her face. "Do you know I never wanted to be a detective?"

"Didn't you?"

"No. I was happy being a cop, visiting schools and the like. They keep pushing you to go further."

That struck her as an odd thing to say. He seemed like the sort of person who would be constantly striving for success. Perhaps he thought that Esther was stuck in a dead-end job and was trying to play the classic "good cop" and identify with her, to get her on-side. Yes, that must be it.

Oh, shut up, Esther, she told herself. *You really are over-thinking things.*

"How come you said you weren't friends with Rochelle?" he asked her.

"Well, she was, you know, Rochelle. No other reason," she added, defensive.

"How would you describe her? Just to help me get a feel for the person, it's not on the record."

"I don't think I knew her that well, but I'd say hard-working and sensible. Direct. She didn't take any rubbish."

"Right. Well, I'd better move on."

He sounded just like a caricature of an English bobby in that moment.

He did have lovely lips, she thought. They were just the right mix of full and thin, and had little light hairs around them. And when he smiled, she melted a little.

But as she followed the winding lane to her work, she thought back over the conversation and became more and more uncomfortable. The way Clark looked at her made her feel like she was stripped bare. Did he suspect her?

She was the one with Rochelle when they walked down the alley. If so, it was even more urgent that she find out what actually happened. She was sure that the homeless man, Raid, would have something useful to add.

She unlocked the shop and turned the sign to 'Open' with a sigh. If the police wouldn't do their job, she would have to step up.

CHAPTER 7

$\mathcal{E}$sther decided she would approach this the same way she learnt about relationships and puberty and learnt to play the ukelele. She pushed the revolving door and stepped into the warmth of the library, in her lunch hour. It was and noisier than usual. Women seated in brightly coloured chairs were discussing something for their book club, and it seemed to be getting quite heated.

Esther put the lime covered Murder Investigation for Dumbos on the self-checkout and scanned her library card. A loud bing-bong noise and orange and red lights flashed around the screen.

"Bing bong? What bing bong?" she muttered.

"Are you alright?" the librarian called from her desk.

She was a young woman in a mustard cardigan and long dark hair.

Esther gathered up her things and went up to the desk. "I was trying to get these books out, but it doesn't like my card."

The librarian raised perfect eyebrows and brushed the green-dyed streak back off her face. "Let's have a look. You might have overdue fines owing."

"I shouldn't."

She waited. The librarian's fingers moved swiftly over the keyboard. "Fifty nine pounds and thirty. You had a book called The Making of a Performer for thirteen weeks."

Her heart sunk. "Oh no, I must have forgotten about it."

"Alright. Look. I don't want people not to have access to books." The librarian leaned forwards. "Especially as I know you're one of our regulars. I'm going to wipe those, as long as you go home and have a really good look for the book. If you find it, bring it back in."

"Thanks!"

She grabbed the bright green book and swiped it through without letting any emotion pass over her face when she saw the title. Esther silently thanked her again.

"Ask for me, Cara. Who am I kidding? I'm usually the only one here, anyway."

"Let's run through once more." Ashton took a sip of water, and sat on the edge of the couch.

Esther rubbed her hands together. "It's sounding good. Mr Bauer might not like us practising for more than half an hour though. It's almost time for Eastenders."

Louis stalked his way into the lounge and sat in the middle of the floor, glaring at Ashton, who moved away.

"Out!" She said to the kitten. She thought about how to bring up what Phoebe had told her about overhearing Ash talking to Rochelle.

"I talked to Jayden today at work," he said, instead, and she was grateful. What a coward she was.

"Oh? What did he say?"

"Not much. He seemed like he didn't want to talk about it. Then he said he had to go to the gym. But I think he's had a fight with his wife."

"Hmm, ok."

Ashton picked up his phone then and swiped across to take a call. Esther looked across the road to the cemetery, where trees waved their bare grey branches in the wind. Flowering rhododendrons showed their red flowers against dark leaves.

"Yes, I'm here. I… what?" Ashton was saying, rubbing his hand hard across his chin.

Esther watched him.

He put his phone back in his pocket. Then picked up his hat and jammed it on his head. "They want to question me about the… body."

He stood up, but didn't seem to know quite where to turn.

"Oh no," Esther said, which felt dumb and awkward. Her insides were currently shooting downwards, so she felt faintly nauseous.

"Someone told them I had a falling out with Rochelle recently. What the hell?"

The blood was pounding in her head.

Esther didn't remember much else from that afternoon, but she somehow found herself at home, with Aria passing her a hot cup of raspberry tea. Since last weekend, she must have drunk a barrel of tea. It felt like so long ago. A lifetime ago.

"Esther, are you there?"

She shook her head. "Ashton!"

"Yes, you keep saying that," her friend said, gently, patting Esther's shoulder. "He's been arrested, but it will all be fine. I know that. You know that."

She took the tea, which somehow seemed to be rattling on its saucer, and placed it on the side table. The orange red liquid smelled delicious and fruity, and one hot sip brought her back to the here and now.

"They have to let him go. We've got to do something."

"They will." Aria took the fluffy wrap off the couch and wrapped it around her shoulders. She put Mamma Mia on the television and sat down beside her. "He'll turn up at your nan's ready for the show, you'll see."

"Oh, while I remember, I've got to ask. Can you ask Troy to chat to Jayden? I think you mentioned they know each other?"

"Yeah, through the gym, I think. Do you suspect him?"

"No, but we are going through all the people we work with, to clear them."

"Okay," Aria said. "Hey, don't worry, Ash will bounce back. You know him."

Esther nodded. "And in the meantime, I have to prove it wasn't him."

CHAPTER 8

That night, when she was alone, distracted and anxious, she wandered over the road.

Esther walked past the church and opened the little gate into the cemetery. Some might think it was a morbid place to be, but it was actually very beautiful, even at this time of the year, with tall firs around the edges, and well-kept rhododendrons, and the bright memorial garden in the middle. There was a spot at the back where she could practise her singing and no one would hear.

She ran her hands over the trunk of the maple, and hummed the Mamas and the Papas song, Autumn Leaves, with a clear memory of the first day she had moved to Ledstow. It was a warm day in November, and her dad and Phillip were carrying her drawers into the flat. She'd had to remove the legs off a table and three people stopped to chat to her.

She heard a crunching noise and looked around to see if someone had snapped a twig. Below her feet were auburn red leaves, crunchy and curled. More were floating gently down, spiralling around her. The tree behind her had lost half its leaves, and grey branches stretched to the sky.

Was she going crazy? She was ninety percent sure the tree hadn't been like that before. But she was always accused of being a dreamer. She checked her phone. It was the 17th of December, so it was full winter. Maybe the leaves had just never fallen off. She looked around, but most of the trees were evergreens. There was one other that was grey and bare. There, a walnut tree.

She looked back, heart beating fast. Had she done that?

No, she thought. That's not possible. She walked between the rows of purple verbena.

There had been other weird happenings, though. The frogs. Was she somehow causing strange, out of season things to happen?

Then there was the cat. Louis hadn't just appeared at her house one day. But it was very close to that.

It was a grey autumn morning about a month ago, when her neighbour, Mr Bauer, ran into her down the street. He was holding a large box with holes in it which he sat down carefully on the footpath when he saw her.

"Mr Bauer," she said, with a smile. "Do you need me to come this week?" Esther sometimes cleaned his house on a Friday, since he found it hard to get down on his hands and knees. She hadn't been to help out for the last few weeks.

"Oh, I could do with your help, actually. I have to take this cat down to the shelter. Could you give me a lift?"

She looked sideways at the box.

"Do you want me to show you?" he asked, raising his eyebrows at her. "It could be dangerous. I know how you melt into a puddle with any cute animals."

She pretended to consider for a moment, just to make him happy. "I think I can handle it," she said, bending down to open the flap.

"Just be careful."

She looked in and saw the cutest grey face looking at her with large eyes. It blinked its eyes against the light.

"Oh you shouldn't be allowed," she said.

"I did try to warn you," he said, smiling down at her. "Looks cute as anything. I can see you melting from here. Do not reach in though!"

"Why not?"

"It'll get you. This one has something wrong with it, I think. I actually can't look after him."

"What do you mean?"

"I came home one afternoon and it had broken two glasses.

Also, it ruined my wife's woollen blanket. I'm too old for such a high maintenance house mate."

Esther's phone went off in her pocket. She picked up the phone and swiped across. Too late, she realized it was her mum. She wasn't in the right frame of mind for this today.

"Oh, you answered," her mother's clipped tones came through the phone. "I was getting ready to leave a message."

"You got me," she sighed.

"Are you still coming for Christmas?" Her mother asked. It was pointed, as if Esther often said she was going to things, then backed out. That wasn't fair, she thought, biting her lip. She usually said she didn't want to go in the first place.

"What? It's ages away. Of course I am."

"I just thought I'd better check, so I know whether I can hire out those two rooms. I've had a reservation come through."

"Oh, alright. And nan is excited about coming."

Her mum made a noise that sounded like hmph.

"Say goodbye," Mr Bauer said, lifting the box up ready to go.

"Who said that?" her mum said. "Who is telling you to hang up on your mother?"

She reached into the box with one hand and the kitten batted at her hand with its paw. What a poor, misunderstood kitten, she thought.

"Hang on, mum," she said, putting her hand over the microphone. "Why are you getting rid of it, again?"

"It's very naughty. It must have been a wild cat. I can't watch it all the time, when I'm out at chess or napping."

Esther made up her mind. She wasn't sure why, but this cat had come to her for a reason. She absolutely couldn't see him go to the pet shelter.

"Leave it with me," she said.

"Are you sure?" Mr Bauer looked at her as if she was a stubborn licorice stuck to the bottom of his tin.

She nodded, and put the phone back to her ear. "What do I need to get to adopt a kitten?"

Her mum sighed. "Where is this coming from? Esther? Do you need to get yourself a boyfriend?"

"No way," she said. "Why is that what you always come back to? I'm going to be a cat lady." She couldn't resist teasing her mum.

"Good grief."

"Litter box, bed, toys, food? What else?"

"Well, you need to make sure it has had its shots. And that it's been fixed." She could almost hear her mum pursing her lips on the other end. "You don't want any babies running around."

She looked down at the box by her feet. Its flaps were moving. "Gotta go, mum. The kitten is escaping..."

Nothing about this was really that strange, she thought. But the timing was. It had happened the same week that Aria moved out, leaving her alone in the flat.

A message from Vicky came through to her phone. She had sent a group email to the staff telling them all to reply with their availability. She wanted to check they were alright after the 'terrible shock'.

Esther eyed the little white ball of fluff that was making a high pitched noise, warily.

Vicky invited her in. "Shoes off, please."

So that was how she kept the cream carpet so immaculate. Esther was sure that it wouldn't last a week at her place.

Vicky looked at her. "I'm just not sure if I'm doing the right thing. Should I open the shop back up? It feels wrong."

"I'm not sure what the right thing is, but people like Phoebe really rely on the income."

"Phoebe?"

"Yeah. And me as well, I suppose."

"True. Roch had everyone on these casual contracts to minimise wages. I can't believe they all stood for it."

"They probably didn't have much say," she said. "It changed there after you left."

Vicky stood up and wandered over to the bookcase. "The partnership works better if we communicate by email. One of us had to go. If not, we'd probably have killed each other." Esther looked up, but she didn't seem to realize what she had said. "I'm not sure if you know, but your friend Ashton does my hair."

"Oh? What is he like as a hairdresser?" Esther eyed Vicky's loose curls. Her hair was a very dark red, almost pink. It suited her. She definitely didn't look the almost sixty years old that she was.

"He's great. I don't even have to tell him what I want anymore. If I tell him I need a change, he'll try something out, and it always looks great."

"I never came into the bookshop that much, since I stepped back from it. But I was due to see Rochelle in the weekend. Ashton didn't seem to be his usual self. He rinsed my hair with lukewarm water, and pulled at it, like his mind was somewhere else. Usually, he would chatter away about his partner's kid and the festivals he was going to go to. He eventually said that Rochelle was blaming him for taking something. He had no idea why she thought it was him. It was a book, I think."

"Oh man." The bichon frise came into the lounge and Esther put her hand down to pat it, which it obviously took as an invitation as it leapt through the air onto her lap. It stood on her legs, wiggling its cloud of a tail. "Woah, hello there."

"Minnie, get down," Vicky said, while Minnie steadfastly ignored her. "I was his last client so I asked him if he wanted to get a drink next door at the Pig and Horse. He told me that he was sure that it was actually Phoebe who had taken the book. Get down, Minnie."

"Really?" Esther couldn't imagine Ashton gossiping

about anyone, let alone ratting someone else out. No matter how upset he was. Were people really that different around others? Did they change their entire personalities?

She shook her head. That was rather a larger problem that would best be mulled over a glass of wine. "You said you were due to see Rochelle..."

"Yes," she said. Esther waited, and Vicky brushed her hair behind her ear. "I was going to show her some of my husband's books. But I called it off. I thought if she wasn't in the right frame of mind, it would be no good. Drew would be so annoyed if I didn't get what his books were worth. What he thought they were worth, anyway."

Esther knew that her husband had passed away, but she didn't know anything else about him. She looked at Vicky with sympathy. "How long has it been?"

"Twelve years this coming February. I still hear his voice in my head every day."

Esther thought back to the stairway and the hall with doors leading off on both sides. It was a big house to live in all alone. She wondered if Vicky had dated anyone else but thought it was probably a bit rude to ask.

"That must be so hard."

"Yeah, I was with him from age fifteen. He was my older brother's friend who we always teased, because of his freckly face."

Esther smiled. Vicky still sounded so tender when she talked about him.

"Anyway, I'm just trying to catch up with each staff member to make sure they are alright. People are our greatest resource."

"Thanks," she said, wishing Vicky was her manager at the music shop instead of Hugh.

"Oh, and a message came through from that customer, Mr Deed. He wants you to go and talk to him."

"Me?" This was getting ridiculous. Perhaps she needed to become a terrible listener, and start judging everyone, so that she wouldn't be traipsing all over town to hear everyone's life stories.

"If you don't feel comfortable, that's fine. I'll just tell him you're too busy."

"I appreciate that," she said. "I'll have a think about it."

The next day, at work, Esther refilled the tea and coffee canisters in the staff room. She pulled out a bag of sugar from the cupboard, and ripped it open.

She was nervous about going to visit Rochelle's husband today with Phoebe. But it would also be good to get a few answers. At the moment, she felt like the person that played the triangle in the orchestra, right at the edge, waiting for her turn.

Esther hoped that the truth would be found in the course of the investigation, and that justice would be served. It had been five endless days so far, and nothing had changed. How long did this sort of thing take? She was sure that the man at the side of the road must know something more. She got the feeling he perceived a lot more than people perhaps gave him credit for.

Her boss was watching some documentary in his office. It droned on and on. "The strongest memories are associated with emotions. When we experience a strong emotion, like joy, love, anger or sadness, the amygdala is stimulated and our memories are sharpened…"

She looked down, and realized she had dumped the sugar into the coffee container. Now, the white was tinged with brown. She sighed.

It seemed like the police weren't doing a good job. They still didn't even know the time of death. She herself wouldn't be that inclined to open up to Detective Norman, if she had anything to confess. She was far too confrontational. And the other one, Clark. He was, perhaps, reluctant to take charge. He seemed almost ashamed to be a policeman. But there was nothing for it.

They had to rely on the police to sort it out. Didn't they?

On Thursday afternoon, Phoebe picked her up from work. "We haven't got long, as the kids are at daycare. Thank you for doing this."

Esther had never seen a man more distraught than Greg

Farmer. He opened the door for them, hunched against his grief, in his dressing gown and slippers. He opened the curtains as they walked through the house, past tables filled with bouquets of flowers. He sat down and two small brown dogs immediately ran in and jumped onto his lap. A third waddled in, and flopped down in a patch of sun.

"Over there," he said, pointing behind where Esther was standing awkwardly. "The top of the stack. I've got more bloody muffins than I know what to do with. Everyone brings them. Help yourselves."

Phoebe passed the plastic container over and Esther took a chocolate muffin and sat down.

"Thank you for coming," he said, running a hand through his hair. "I can't seem to settle to anything, so it's nice to have someone here." He sighed. "They want me to make decisions about the funeral."

"It's still early days," Esther said, gently.

"Greg, are you eating properly?" Phoebe asked. "Are you going back to work?"

"My boss has been really good," he said, picking up a muffin and turning it round, as if it was a foreign object. "Too good, really. I need to go back to the factory to keep the old mind going."

"Give yourself a few more days." Phoebe flicked the jug on and opened cupboard doors, looking for cups.

"We wanted to talk to you about the bookshop,"

Esther said. She took her hair out, and re-plaited it, for something to keep her hands busy.

"And… and Rochelle," Phoebe added.

"She was such a jewel, that woman. Shone everywhere she went."

"She must have been different at home than at work," Esther said, then clapped her hand to her mouth, as she realized what she had said. Phoebe glanced over.

Greg didn't seem to notice, as he continued on, waving in the direction of a glittery silver Christmas tree in the corner. "She's in every single decoration on that tree. I don't even want to look at it. We've got a big dog show coming up, too, but the dogs aren't interested. They are mourning too."

"What do you think is going to happen with the shop?" Phoebe tried again. Her long hair swung as she placed the tea onto the table next to Greg. "I put a little milk in for you."

"Thanks, love. Sell it, I suppose, and get nothing at all. I'll have to talk to Vicky at some stage. It could even owe us money, with all the dough she spent on making it look fancy. I don't really care about that, right now."

"Of course not. What do you think… I mean…" Esther trailed off, and an uncomfortable silence lengthened. She looked away, kicking herself for starting to ask the question.

"It's alright," he said, and stood up to look out the window. The two dogs jumped off and went over to Phoebe. "Everybody has asked me, from the chap at the pizza store to the next door neighbour. I know beyond a doubt that it wasn't a medical issue. I made her get checked over a while ago. I was more worried about her than she was."

Esther sipped her tea, which was unbelievably hot. She licked her stinging lip. "So do you think… someone else was involved? Because the alternative is…"

In her own mind, Esther was positive that Rochelle wasn't depressed. But you never knew. She felt sick to her stomach at having to ask, but she had to see what he thought.

She heard a thunk, and Greg stepped back. "Jeez. A bird just hit the window. Oh no, wait, the bloody thing is standing up, but it's a bit dazed. Like me, at the moment." He laughed to himself. "I think it'll be alright."

Phoebe brought the muffins over again and offered them to Greg. "These are good. Have another. I see you're on the Market committee," she said, waving her hand at some papers. "I've got a stall there." Esther had to hand it to her that she knew how to make people feel comfortable. A cup of tea. Some baking. Common ground.

"Yes, we used to have a stall selling dog collars and leads. Roch liked the glitzy ones."

Esther smiled at Greg. "You were saying?"

He shook his head. "Don't you think I've thought it all

over a hundred times? There's no way on earth that she would ever do that."

"Why?"

"Because she told me every day that she was having the best time of her life. I just wish we'd found each other earlier." His voice broke a little.

Esther finished her tea, which was only now at a drinkable temperature. She collected up the cups, making sure not to fall over the small, snuffling dogs who raced around her into the kitchen.

"Phoebe is wondering about her course, as well," she ventured. "Will that be paid for?"

"Course? Certainly. We will honour that for whatever you agreed."

Phoebe grinned. "Thank you. That means so much to me."

"We made a lot more out of the dog collar stall than we ever got out of the bookshop, you know. She ended up hating it, I think."

"Would you know of anybody who'd have anything against her? Any arguments? Any disputes over money?"

"Are you joking? That woman was Mother bloody Theresa. Best three years of my life."

Esther smiled, but didn't trust herself to open her mouth.

"The only person who wasn't totally in love with her was her ex husband, Bobby. Grumpy git, that guy."

As he closed the door behind them, after having made them promise to come back and visit, she looked at Phoebe.

"Were we talking about the same Rochelle?" she whispered.

"Bless him. He's a lovely man and you can see he loves her from the bottom of his heart." She opened the door of her little Fiat.

Esther climbed in. She was happy that their visit seemed to have removed two possible options. It was less encouraging that murder was the only option left.

Rochelle didn't deserve to be attacked, just because she had a brash demeanour — no, a demeanour that could freeze the balls off a brass monkey. Rochelle was a wife and a dog owner. She was a daughter, and probably a sister, auntie, and cousin.

She wondered about the ex husband and what reason he would have. And why now? And she thought she could definitely count Greg out.

"Love is blind, as they say," she said to Phoebe.

The pub was called The Twig and Berries, which Esther found amusing, but no-one else seemed to notice. There was always the same group of half a dozen locals at the table in the corner. She felt drawn to the roaring fire immediately and stopped to warm her hands before going up to the bar.

"Evening," said the bartender, a wiry man with a heavily pierced nose and lower lip.

She ordered a mulled wine, mouth watering in expectation of the spicy sweet drink. "Can I get a menu please?"

"For you, I'd recommend the Beef Wellington." He twirled a glass around and pointed it at her, then gave it a quick swish with a tea towel.

She never usually ordered red meat, preferring chicken or vegetarian food. But tonight, Beef Wellington sounded perfect.

"Yes, I will have that, thanks." She found a table in the corner.

Aria arrived shortly after, wearing a beautiful lambswool dress, and carrying a glass of red. "I just ordered the chicken," she said. "The bartender was writing it down before it even came out of my mouth, though."

"This town," Esther said, shaking her head. "Where's Troy?"

"He should be here soon. He has to go home and shower after football training."

"I'm just wearing my jacket and look at you."

"Why, thank you."

"I really wanted to chat to you about this whole…" She waved her hand around in a circle.

"Murder thing?" Aria whispered.

Esther tipped her cup up and felt the liquid warm her all the way down. "Yeah. Phoebe is acting really weird, but I doubt she would have it in her. She did say she felt like a little voice was telling her off, though."

"Really?" Aria took a sip of her wine.

"Yeah. And people keep telling me things about Ash that don't sound like him at all."

"Like what?"

"Oh, that he got angry at Rochelle. That he gossipped about Phoebe."

Aria looked off into the distance. "We have to trust what our mate says, I think. I always get a feeling about people and he is one of the best sorts."

"You're right, of course."

"Look, do you think you should be getting involved? I know it's exciting, but…"

"I definitely do," she said "Now would you like a mulled wine?"

She ordered the drinks and waited next to the fire until they were ready.

Grabbing the cups, she heard a familiar voice. Down the other end of the bar was the policeman, Clark. He was talking on his phone, voice low. She put up her hood and slid quietly down towards him.

"Yes, I've questioned Jayden, and his alibi checks out. His wife told us that he was at home that night."

She inched closer. "We've talked to that homeless man twice now. He doesn't know anything. And Jo wasn't there. It really leaves Ashton, Vicky, the cleaner and Esther. And the victim's husband, of course."

"No, I don't think it was her."

Who was he talking about? He started turning around and she turned the other way. She looked up and found herself staring right into the eyes of the bartender.

"No hoods inside," he said, but he looked as if he was trying not to laugh.

She hurried off and put the cups down on their table, then took her hood off. She had only spilled a little bit on her hand.

"What was that all about?" Aria asked.

"Never mind," she said. But she knew what she had to do next.

CHAPTER 10

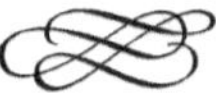

It was a day later that Esther approached the man in the park. She chose the large tea rooms in the middle of town, across the road from the gate to the park. She ordered two extra large cappuccinos and a banana choc chip muffin dripping with icing, and took the number over to the table by the window.

"Thank you for coming," she said. She felt a little nervous, but she wasn't going to let it bother her.

Raid was sitting with his faded blue jacket zipped up and hands folded on his lap. He looked up at her.

"What's this about, lady?"

"I'm Esther."

"Are you just doing your good deed for Christmas-time? That's what people do. They give us a free

Christmas lunch and then forget about us for the rest of the year."

"That's... awful." She was struck again by the kind blue eyes, now creased with humour.

The waitress brought over the drinks and the muffin, and Esther offered it to him. "Do you want something to eat?"

He shook his head. "No, it's not. It's just people. Thanks for the drink," he said, lifting the coffee to his mouth and taking a hearty gulp. "Sometimes it's hard for others to see people like us. Really see us. Makes them feel uncomfortable."

"Did you grow up here?"

"Yeah, I'm Ledstow born and bred. I did go off and spend some time in Italy when I was young."

"Did you?" She was completely taken by surprise.

He chuckled. "I love doing that to people," he said, waving his hand around. "That feeling? That's your judgements about me getting turned on their heads. It's a bit sickening, isn't it?"

She nodded. "Sorry."

"I studied Law at uni as well. Never passed the bar exam, though. Thought I'd chuck it all in after that, and go live down at the park. Well, I started off here and moved around to other towns, other parks, other beaches. Ended up here again. Something always brings me back to the cobbled alleys and the scent of baking bread. There's just something about this place. Sometimes it takes one unexpected event to change your whole life's trajectory."

"That's one hell of a story," she said, shaking her head. And quite poetic, she thought.

"That's not even half of it," he said. His expression grew guarded. "Are you a journalist or something?"

"No. I am just... a friend of the woman who passed away. I wanted to check if you knew anything else. I heard that talking to the police didn't go that well," she added softly.

"It went well for me. Every time they want to talk to me, I get a doughnut and a cup of tea." Raid grinned.

"Well, it was last Friday night, that really freezing night. Do you remember I crossed the road and dropped some money in your bucket. There was a squirrel."

His expression cleared as he recalled. "The squirrel, yes. But I know what people like me are to the police. Don't mean much at all. Don't have an address, might as well not be a person."

"I'm not them," she said, firmly. "I really just want to get to the bottom of it all." She ate half of the muffin and left half of it there on the plate, feeling intensely guilty, but she had had a large breakfast.

"I do remember two women from that night. One of them almost got knocked over and I thought 'what an idiot.'"

Esther shrugged uncomfortably, remembering the swish of wind and adrenalin spike as the cyclist whooshed past. "Okay. Keep going."

"But after she left, I saw the other one turn back the way they came, the one with short hair. Which I thought was a bit odd."

Esther's breath drew in sharply. That was very odd, indeed. She hadn't noticed Rochelle turn back, but there was only one person inside the bookshop after all the rest of them left. Wasn't there?

"We'd just left Book Ends. Do you think she went back in?"

"It did seem like she had forgotten something. Or someone. Whoever was left behind there, that's who you need to be talking to."

"Did you tell that to the police?"

"No, I p-p-play my role with them. Don't tell them nuthin'. Now when are you going to come and visit us down at the park?"

"Hmm. Well."

"I'm joking. Relax," he said. "You could say hi when you walk past next time, though." He pulled the plate towards him, and stuffed the half muffin into his mouth.

CHAPTER 11

Once Raid ambled over the road back to the park, Esther went outside. She sat down at one of the tables, pushing the dishes from the last occupants to the middle, and pulled out her notebook, checking around behind her. A tapping came from the ground. She looked down at the bird that was pecking around. There must be crumbs down there.

"I've seen you before, haven't I?" Esther said quietly. There was something about the bird that made her want to talk to it. "But you all look the same, so it could quite easily be a different jay." It ruffled its feathers up and flew up onto the edge of the table.

The bird walked forward, stretched its neck out and grabbed a little piece of bread off the edge off the plate. She put a hand flat on the table, keeping still as it looked at her out of its beady eye, and leaned down to nip her finger.

"Ow," she said, and the bird hopped back a step. She lifted her finger up to look at it. It hadn't drawn blood. "What did you do that for?"

It hopped along the edge of the table. Then it bobbed its head and puffed up its feathers.

"You are the same one? You don't like me talking loud?" It came forwards two little jumps, almost like it could understand her. Like *it* was training *her*.

"I will talk calmly in a low voice like this," she said, and the bird continued its advance. "I will keep my hand flat on the table."

She looked behind her to see if anyone was watching. When she looked back, it was staring right at her with one beady eye, head cocked on the side.

"You can trust me, birdie."

It jumped onto her hand and clung on with scratchy feet, and jumped up towards her arm. Esther started getting nervous. What was it trying to do?

She kept her voice low, and murmured, "What are you after? I have to go back to work."

Louder, she said, "Fly away. Come on." She shook her hand a little, but it didn't want to get off. "Oh no, I am not taking you back to Guitar Pharaoh!"

But no matter how hard she shook her arm, it didn't leave.

A jingle made Esther look up at the door. She glanced over at the drumkit in the window, where the bird was perched, watching.

"I'd like to talk to you," Clark said. He marched toward her and took his hat off.

Esther's heart sped up and her palms turned clammy. Was he here to arrest her? Question her about Ashton? She grabbed onto the edge of the bench to steady herself.

"What's this?"

"I just want to chat," he said. "When is your break?"

"I should be able to take it in about ten minutes," she said, slowly. I'll just check that the boss will be here."

"I'll be here," Hugh called. He was obviously listening from his office, while watching his documentaries. "You just do whatever you need to."

Clark suppressed a smirk. "I'll meet you at the café then, Grounds for Divorce, in about fifteen minutes?"

She nodded, and it was only as he turned to leave that she let herself truly panic. She had assumed that she would be questioned about Ashton at some point. All the feelings of guilt for undertaking her own investigation were bringing her anxieties up.

By the time she got to the café, she was in just about the same state as the first time she had been there.

She ordered herself a pot of tea, so that it would give

her something to do with her hands. She didn't think she would be able to stomach any. The top of her scalp was prickling and she fumbled with her wallet when getting her card out and had to put the pin in twice.

"You're welcome." Lottie winked at her.

"What for?" Esther asked. She was distracted, looking around the room for Clark.

Lottie placed a pebble painted with the number 8 on the counter. "For that lovely man," she said, cryptically.

Esther raised her eyebrows. "Oh no, we're not on a—"

"Over here," Clark said, from behind her.

Esther gratefully grabbed the stone and placed it in the middle of the table.

She sat down facing Clark and took a deep breath. "Ashton absolutely didn't do it." The words came out louder than she intended. Her hands were curled into fists at her side.

Clark put his hands out in front of him. "I know," he said.

"There is absolutely no way. He is the most—"

"I know," he interrupted. "Is he your boyfriend?"

Esther looked up at him, shocked, as the information finally got through to her brain. He wasn't trying to get information from her about her friend. But he was asking her personal questions about herself now. She sat down automatically. "What?"

"I'm sorry," he said. "I shouldn't have asked that."

"No, you probably shouldn't."

The waitress brought the tea over. He looked at her, his intense gaze flicking over her eyes, jaw, shoulders, hands. His hands were flat on the table.

"Are you alright?" he said.

She nodded, then picked up the pot and poured out a generous cup, adding just a tiny splash of milk. "You?"

"Yes. You don't trust me, do you?"

"Should I?" Esther knew she was being rude at this point, but something about him rubbed her up the wrong way.

"I wanted to chat to you today, because I worked out that it wasn't Ashton. He simply doesn't have the motive. Shona doesn't think I'm right. Sometimes, her focus seems like it is guilty until proven innocent, that one. Just between you and me," he added quickly.

"Well, that's good." she said, a bit lamely. "So you can help me prove he's innocent?"

"I also… I also know you've been looking into things yourself, Esther."

"Sorry?" she asked, on edge again.

"Don't worry. I was thinking that maybe we could work together on this. You're making real progress. You seem like you're really into researching. Like me."

'How did you find out?"

"You're always appearing in the same places as me." He counted the reasons on his fingers. "Some of the suspects I spoke to had already spoken to a woman with brown hair, who came along asking questions. They never told me her name." He was grinning. "But it didn't take a genius."

She licked her lips. "Oh. Did you go to the funeral?"

"I parked nearby just to watch. Nothing really untoward. I thought I'd see you there."

"How did Greg seem?"

He seemed surprised. "Greg? The husband? I don't know. Broken, I guess." He looked at his phone. "I suppose you've got to get back now?"

He drank the rest of his tea in one gulp.

She flicked over her phone to check. "Oh, yes! I do!"

Esther walked back to work, a spring in her step as she passed the lines of quaint stone houses in the old town, feeling lucky to live in beautiful Ledstow. If Clark wanted to work together, that meant that he needed her. And she had the perfect job for him to do first.

"Are you alright to wait out here?"

"Sure. I don't have anything better to do," Clark joked, sitting with one leg out of the car. He was wearing jeans and a polo shirt today, and she thought he looked much more approachable than the blue uniform.

"It'll probably be fine, but I feel a lot better having

someone close by. I'd say I'll be about fifteen minutes." He'd been happy enough to go along with the plan, but had taken a bit of convincing that she shouldn't wear a recording device.

"I didn't know whether I should say anything, lass," Mr Deed said, bringing the cup of tea over and placing it in front of her. "You're all so busy, and I did try to get hold of you early on. Then I thought, 'no, they don't need to hear an old codger's ramblings.'"

"Oh, we do, Mr Deed," Esther said. She took a sip and the hot tea stung her lip, so she quickly put it down again. She felt a bit guilty that they had just thought that he wanted to hang out in the shop. "Happy to chat to a fellow reader."

"Call me Harry, eh. I'm normally looking for manuals in the bookshop. Well, I've got quite a lot of time on my hands and never fancied myself the retired sort of chap. I do a bit of amateur tinkering, you see. Fixing things up. I've got a whole shed full of all sorts of things out the back, like old typewriters, mowers, even a couple of old engines. I go around a few garage sales and find stuff, interesting bits and bobs. When Dee was around, she used to like looking at the house things. I fixed up a cake mixer for her."

His face fell. Esther followed his glance to the wedding photograph on the mantelpiece.

"That's very clever of you," she prompted, gently.

"I just love finding out what makes things tick. And the people you meet, some of them have some interesting stories. But I can't go far, and nobody reads the papers anymore. So where do you sell things?"

"Mm." Esther reached for a biscuit. This could take a while. She would need to keep her strength up.

"So my son got me onto this community page. I can do my fixing up and selling and put it on there, easy. Then someone comes by the next day to pick it up... and Bob's your uncle, as they say. Had a fellow come over this morning to pick up the lawn mower I fixed up. 'Good as new', I said. 'Probably last you another thirty years.' Ended up finding him a beer keg too. Then he said he was looking for a bike seat, so I showed him some of those."

He must have mistaken her eyes glazing over for the shine of excitement. "I can take you out there for a look around, if you like," he said.

She held up the tea cup, which was nearly finished, indicating she had to drink it while it was hot. "So, about the case?"

"Case? Ah, well, the lady from the bookshop is on that community group, but it's not under her name. I know that because once someone asked for a rearview mirror. What do you know? I had the exact one. It was her that turned up to pick it up. Paid me the twenty pounds and was off on her way. It's Pete Pages."

Esther privately doubted it had been anything like that fast, but then again, Rochelle could be pretty blunt.

"Was that what you wanted to tell me?"

"What? No, I'm not nearly up to that yet. Sometimes I read the community page just to see what people are talking about. Well, not talking so much as yelling at each other. Can you imagine if people did that in the street? I saw that blighter Pete Pages get involved in a bit of a stramash, so that got me interested." He leaned forward, fiddling with the novelty teaspoon which had a miniature gondola inside it. "Somebody posted that a dog did its business on their lawn and urged the council to fine them. They swore black and blue that it was this particular dog. Pete Pages just said they were crazy. But then other people started digging in, telling them that it was disgusting."

"Ugh, that's awful."

He tipped the teaspoon up and the gondola went floating down to the bottom. "So, I don't know if it's got anything to do with it, but I just thought I'd let you know, since I saw you at the shop with your wee notebook."

"Yeah, I'm not sure if it's relevant, either." There certainly were a few people who had gotten into stramashes with Rochelle. She flicked over her phone. She had already been in there for twenty minutes. "But thanks for telling me."

"Come on, I'll show you my shed," he said, again. "Come on, girl."

Esther had to admire his enthusiasm, at least. She followed him down the back steps and out onto the path. A little gate led straight onto the river and a path wound around alongside it. It was almost sickeningly beautiful. A huge old shed stood to the left with cobwebs in the windows.

"Wow."

Harry nodded.

"Do you know who the other person was? Who first posted about the... er, mess?"

He opened the door of the shed, and stood aside. "It was a cartoon face, not a real person's face, and the name was Donald Drew or something like that. Drew Donald?"

"Okay, thank you. Um, how come you didn't go to the police?" she asked, carefully. The inside was packed to the brim apart from a small path down the middle. In the gloom, she could see old rusted prams, electronic keyboards with missing keys and a retro fridge with colourful kilts draped over top.

"Them? Nah. I used to be a used car salesman back in the day and I've had a few run-ins with them. They always barged in without knowing the, ah, nuance of a situation."

Esther cringed. So this Harry had found himself on

the wrong side of the law? She found herself wondering whether she could trust what he said.

"It was years ago. Gave it all up when Dee asked me to. Small price to pay, really."

She nodded. "Well, I better…"

"You're a top girl, you are, Esther. I'll make sure to chat to you whenever I come into Book Ends."

"Lovely," she said. Although she might need to set an egg timer so she got some work done too, she was surprised to find that she meant it.

She went back out to the car and Clark looked up, relieved.

"I checked at the window a couple of times. I was just planning what to do next, since I didn't see you in there the last time."

"He's a talker, but harmless, I think. He showed me his shed."

Clark snorted. "What is that supposed to mean?"

"Exactly what I said."

"So what next then?"

She shook her head. "You're the cop. You tell me. Where have your investigations got to?"

"Well, I'm looking into this one person," he said. "She's got long, brown hair and a cute laugh, and she always pauses before speaking, like she's thinking carefully."

She smiled. "That is not professional," she said.

"I can't help it."

"Look, it's a rule. I don't go out with policemen."

"Okay," he said, putting his hands up.

In the car on the way back home, she reflected on the weird things that had happened. It seemed like it was every time she sang. People falling asleep. Frogs that had come out of the ground. Had Clark suspected that it was her? As well as having a malfunctioning immune system and a uterus that wanted to claw its way out of her for a week each month, she now had a wacky season generator? Just what she needed. What even was that? It wasn't even useful.

After he dropped her off, she called her nan. The phone rang and rang, and she realized it was bingo time. She smothered a smile, thinking of Kevin and Hope frantically stamping their numbers.

"Hello, my lovely nan," she started, when she heard the beep. "Odd things are happening all around me, and I'd like you to tell me why," she said in a firm voice. It was time for some answers.

CHAPTER 12

*E*sther took the bus out to her nan's rest home. It saved money and the environment. She fiddled with her bag strap and debated with herself whether to go. It wasn't a question of whether she could play the music by herself, but whether she should.

She sighed and pulled out her phone to listen to the voice message. It was from Vicky.

I hope everyone is going okay. Let's open the shop up at ten on Monday. I know it feels pretty weird right now, but at least we can talk to each other about it. And it will give us something to focus on. I've been in touch with Rochelle's husband, so I can pay the wages on Thursday.

So we'll see... Jo, Jayden and me at 10am Monday, and Esther, we'll need you to come in at twelve. Buckle up, as I'm sure it will be busy.

That was something to deal with after the weekend. She stepped off the bus and adjusted her bag. She could do this.

The receptionist waved her through, and her nan was waiting in the small lounge off the hall.

"Are you okay, dear?" Hope asked, when she saw her face.

"I am," she answered, firmly, to make herself believe it. "You know what happened to Rochelle? Ashton has been taken in for questioning."

"Oh dear," her nan said, and pursed her lips. "What are we going to do about that?"

Esther smiled gratefully at her nan, who was draped in a huge bright purple scarf today. Her makeup was done immaculately, as usual, and her arms were dripping in silver bracelets, which clinked as she threw them around Esther and drew her in for a hug. She was always about the action, not dwelling on the problem.

"I'm talking to people as much as I can, but I'm not sure who is telling the truth and who isn't. It doesn't seem like there's much I can do."

Her nan pulled away, and looked up into Esther's face.

"No. Not right now, at any rate. But you can go out there and play some lovely music. He would want you to do that anyway."

"Yeah." She was right, of course. Ashton always pushed

her when it came to her singing. "You can always come and perform again."

Hope sat down near the front. There were about twenty people watching from squashy beige armchairs. Esther decided to start off with Little Drummer Boy, then a nice slow version of White Christmas that they had practised. Next she moved onto Do They Know it's Christmas?

She put her ukulele down, and took a sip from her water bottle, eyeing the folk in the room. Some of the staff members were standing against the walls, arms crossed. Perhaps this was a bad idea, after all.

Her eyes fell onto her nan, who was smiling so wide, creases in the edges of her eyes, and nudging her neighbour, as if to say, 'look at that, that's my granddaughter.'

She picked up her ukulele, held it close and strummed some experimental chords.

"Does anyone like country rock?" she said, and a few people looked over. One clapped politely. She played Sweet Home Alabama, then Peaceful, Easy Feelin'.

They were some of her favourites. But she wasn't quite feeling it. She thought of Ashton's mellow voice singing Love Me Do, and wondered how he was doing. Was he singing where he was? Would they let him out soon?

She forced herself to keep her mind on what she was doing, but it was having an effect on her voice, which became strained and thin. She listened to herself, and thought it sounded pathetic, as if she was pleading for someone to love her.

A man struggled up from his chair. "I want my dinner," he said, in a loud voice.

"It's only 4:30, Kevin," one of the nurses said. Esther stopped playing, and in the quiet, heard the screech of cats fighting outside the window.

"Oh, lovely," said the woman next to her nan, starting to push herself up. "Dinner time. I think it's roast pork today." Her nan reached up and tugged at the woman's sleeve to sit back down.

Esther spoke directly to the man. "We're not quite finished yet. About ten minutes more."

Another man, who was very skinny and wearing a red cardigan, said, "Where's Dennis?"

"He's on holiday, Grant," said one of the carers. "As much as we love you all, we do need holidays."

Hope stood up. "My granddaughter is not finished. Please remain seated and enjoy the rest of the show. Now Kevin, do you have a song you'd like to request?"

"Well, I've always liked Walk The Line by Johnny Cash. Can she play that?"

Her nan looked at her. Esther looked back. The room fell still, waiting for her to make a decision.

Her nan opened her mouth, and Esther thought she was going to tell her to hurry up. Instead, Hope sang the first few notes of the guitar melody in a high, clear voice. The whole room turned to look at her. Again, she sang the first few bars, and smiling, put her hand out to Esther, as if to give her the song as a gift.

Esther opened her mouth, copied the notes, and the lyrics came into her head. By the end of the song, everyone was clapping along, and singing with her. They all looked so happy. She finished by walking into the middle of the room, repeating the chorus one last time and putting her arm around her grandmother's shoulders.

"Wow, nan," she said, and clapped up high, signalling that everyone should applaud for Hope as well.

Her nan shrugged and smiled at her, and they walked together down the corridor.

"Okay, don't hold out on me. I knew you were the best nan ever. But I didn't know you could sing like that!"

Her nan flicked her hand at her, and her ring sparkled in the light. "Oh, you knew I loved singing. I used to sing to you all the time." She opened the door to her room, and went inside.

"Yeah, you did," Esther said slowly, packing her ukulele into the case she had painted with flowers. It was coming back to her gradually that her nan would sing to teach her about things, like space or the lifecycle of a butterfly. A caterpillar hangs upside down, she'd sing, and wait for Esther to repeat the tune.

"Why haven't you sung for so long, though?"

"Oh, we grow and things change. Nobody wants to hear oldies sing."

Esther put her hands on her hips. "Um, excuse me, how old are the Rolling Stones?"

Her nan made a noise that sounded a lot like hmmph. "Well, perhaps. It got a bit tense for a while there. Someone had to get the residents into line. Excuse the pun."

"You did great. And puns are always allowed." Her smile was reflected on her nan's face.

"Now, I'll be going to eat dinner soon, dear. Kevin will probably want to sit next to me tonight and he always gives me his roast pumpkin."

Esther recognized the sign to go. "I'll see you again, soon."

Her nan held her fingers with her cool, soft hand. "Don't fall into the worry-well, love. It's too hard to see the answers from down there."

Esther kissed her nan on her soft cheek, and closed the door quietly. As she walked out, she wondered what exactly had just happened. Her nan had saved the gig from total disaster, in one fell swoop uniting a crowd of disgruntled, stressed-out people and turning them into a smiling, singing voice.

She had a lot to learn. But her first problem was

Ashton. Her nan was right. There was no use dwelling on the problem. What on earth was she going to do?

That night, she asked Aria to come over.

"I'm so glad you're here."

"I am too. Troy is out playing poker with the lads. And while I like watching my shows when I'm home alone, I'd much rather be over here with you and this little baby pookums."

Louis rolled onto his back and batted at her hands with soft paws. For some reason, the kitten was like putty in Aria's hands. She ruffled his tummy and he let his head fall back to look at Esther, as if to say, 'look at me'.

"Traitor," she said to him.

The kitten stretched over Aria's lap like a fur blanket. Her eyes flicked over to Esther. "I'm going to set up a dating profile for you."

"No, you aren't." She lunged for her friend's phone but Aria's long arm lifted it out of her reach. "I'm not going out with anyone. I don't have time for that rubbish."

"You have to make time."

"And if I don't want to?" she asked. "What if I spend all my time getting to know them and they turn out to be a lying fool?"

Aria poured herself a glass of wine, and took a sip. "I don't care who it is, you just need someone. Because when I steal this fluffy little ball of cuteness away, you'll be all on your lonesome."

Esther did a half smile. "I don't want to stress out, trying to make small talk with anyone. Full stop."

"Alright, alright," her friend said, as if to placate her, putting her hand out between them. "I'll make up a last name for you."

Esther swiped the phone off her, and put it on the side table.

"Besides, I'm actually really busy at the moment. I've got to figure out who killed Rochelle."

"Do you, really?"

"Well, what if other people are in danger?"

"You don't think there's a serial killer in Ledstow, do you?" Her friend leaned forward, a smile on her face, but she had a glint in her eye.

"What is wrong with you?" Esther shook her head. "No, of course I don't."

Aria crossed her legs on the couch. "Once, at the hotel, a staff member randomly quit and we never saw her again. Later on it turned out she had stolen a ring from a guest's room. So you have to see who would have the most to gain. Follow the money."

Esther shrugged. "That's actually smart. I have no idea. Her husband? Business partner?"

Remembering that Rochelle had had reason not to give the promotion to Ashton, she wondered what had prompted that.

"I think you should try to find that out next. Who has the most to gain from it?"

"I'm not sure, actually, but I think Jo would know."

"Hey, Jo, can we catch up over coffee?"

Jo was looking up some stock on the computer, biting their lip as they scrolled through the list. They lifted up their glasses, checking if they could see any better, then put them back down again.

"It would be too easy if the stock on hand matched, wouldn't it?" they mumbled. "Sorry, when do you mean?"

"Tonight after work?"

Jo flicked their choppy bob out of their face. "I've got quilt club tonight, but you're welcome to come along if you like."

Quilt club. Could it sound any more boring? But Esther knew how busy Jo was, so this might be her best chance to talk to them.

"Yes, alright. Where and when?"

Esther ducked into the coffee shop later that evening. The gas fireplace was roaring in the corner and there was a tinkling of teacups from the back room. The tables had all been pushed back to the walls and chairs were set up in a semicircle.

Esther was surprised to see Lottie, the friendly barista from the coffee shop.

"Hi there," said Lottie. "Have we got a new recruit?" She glanced up without missing a stitch.

"Don't make it sound like a cult," said Jo, in an exaggerated whisper.

Lottie let out a laugh. "Sorry. I'll wait till her second visit for the initiation. We started this club up around twenty years ago, and it's still going strong. I forget it can seem a bit weird to outsiders coming in."

"I only come along for the supper." A man, that she recognised from the petrol station, was sitting in the corner, watching a video on his phone.

"That's Bruce. He's in the Heritage Society as well." Jo put their hand up to cover their mouth but a yawn snuck through.

"This is Moran." A tiny man waved out at her from across the room. "And his wife, Joanie."

"Are you interested in quilting, then, dear?" Joanie was barely visible in her wheelchair beneath a huge green quilt, which was spread across her knees and across her husband's lap. He was holding his hand out to keep the edge of it off the ground.

"I'll give it a go," she said.

A beautiful older woman with skin like paper, who seemed vaguely familiar, spread her square of fabric out on her knee. "Look at this beauty."

"Very nice," she said.

"I'm Iris."

"Oh," Esther said, smiling as she realized who the woman was. "You live at Zany Grey's?"

"Yes, Bruce picks me up each week," she said. "And this is Cara."

Esther waved to the librarian.

"Have a seat," Jo said. "Did you bring your own kit?"

"No I didn't," she said.

"Well, you can use mine," said Jo, offering her a needle. Jo crouched next to Esther and showed her how to cut the fabric and the backing. "We do most of it at home on the machines but there's something... special about doing the work by hand when we come here. This is really my one quiet time. Jayden was so down in the dumps today at work. He said his wife got angry at him for something he did in her dream."

Esther snorted, and looked over at Jo's practised hand. If the mangled Barbie clothes Esther had sewn when she was younger were anything to go by, she needed any help she could get.

Lottie stood up. "I'm just going to get the supper. I'll be back in five."

"Thank the Gods," Bruce called.

Esther struggled to get her needle through the layers of fabric. She looked across at Jo. This was the time to bring it up. Oh, this felt so awkward. She took a deep breath.

"It's so terrible about Rochelle," she murmured. "I feel so bad for her husband."

The skillful hands paused only to take out a pin and place it in the box. "I still can't believe it."

"Do you know if she owned the shop herself?"

"I think it was split between Vicky, Rochelle, and her husband, Greg. Vicky bought into it to keep it afloat a while back."

"I thought so. And Vicky still manages it. I know there's no love lost between them, though. And what will happen to the shop now?"

"It sounds like Greg is going to sell it to Vicky."

When Lottie returned with a tea tray and a huge plateful of baking, she sat down with a meringue. Esther made herself an instant coffee in a large mug and took a piece of carrot cake. She could see why people came for the food. But the companionable crafting was surprisingly pleasant too.

"Did you hear about Rochelle Farmer?" Lottie asked.

Esther became a little uncomfortable.

"We worked with her," Jo explained.

"Oh, of course. I used to babysit her many years ago," said Lottie. "Stubborn kid, and a bit moody. Good heart, ultimately, though."

"Does everyone know everyone in this town?" Esther burst out.

"Pretty much, dear. How long have you lived here?"

"It must be coming up two years in January. I moved here because my Nan is at Greenvale Care just up the road."

Lottie nodded comfortably. "What a lovely grand-daughter. We approve."

"Yes, very good," Iris added.

"You know, I also babysat Jason Sutton."

"The mayor?"

"Little so-and-so, he was. Once peed on my handbag. He was old enough to know better at the time, too."

Jo stood up and walked across the room. "Are you done with your square?"

"Almost," said Moran.

"Oh, you have so. Stop fiddling with it," said his wife, snatching it off him.

"It's not the tv remote," he said, snatching it back.

"Alright," said Lottie loudly. "So then we sew these together, Esther."

She set the nine squares out on one of the tables at the side and Esther could see the blues, greens and golds form into a pattern with a beautiful blue ribbon flowing diagonally through the rows.

"And that's it, until next week. We'll do the final

sewing at our next group. I'll have to check exactly, but I think it's the 22nd."

Esther thought that was a little odd. She didn't know what day they met?

"Do you have someone to go home to, dear?" Joanie asked.

"Just my kitten," she said, privately glad that she hadn't asked if she had a husband. Esther didn't have any strong feelings about getting married, but she did have strong feelings about being asked if she was married. As if it was a foregone conclusion.

"Well, everybody needs someone. Even old Moran here will do, I suppose." She patted him on the knee and he trapped her hand with his.

"Bye, love. Come back again."

Esther helped Jo to pack up their bits and pieces into a giant fabric bag. She looked back as she was heading to the car. Some sixth sense told her that they were talking about her.

CHAPTER 13

*E*sther was standing in front of the fridge, contemplating what to make for dinner. The fridge, as always, did not respond, though the door did creak slightly as she opened it. There were tomatoes, eggs, cheese and milk in there, and that was about it. She pulled things out, and found a pan to make an omelette.

That scratching came again. She really had to get the landlord to do something about the mice.

She broke the eggs and added milk, whipping it up as she sung a song to herself. She placed it on the oven, and a lovely homely smell rose up around her.

She carried the pan over to the bench and flipped it sideways onto the plate. As she did, a terrible thwack came at the window, and she jumped. The omelette flopped half off the plate.

"What is it now?"

Esther went over to the window and looked out. She gasped. A bird was lying on the window ledge outside.

Esther found some gloves to pick up the bird. She heaved the old window up and freezing air came in. Shivering, she placed the bird onto a towel on the coffee table. The poor thing. Birds didn't often hit the window here, as there was only a narrow gap between the two buildings and her window was small.

She turned away to put the gloves in the bin and then came back to shut the window. The bird was struggling to get to its feet. It walked a few steps, waddling along as if dizzy, stuck its beak out and flopped over again.

"Hello, wee birdie. Just rest," she said, using the towel to put under its head.

She moved the magazine away from its head, holding it by its spine and something slipped out onto the floor. She took both over to the bin. She wasn't interested in the magazine at all, so she dropped it in and let the folded paper fall on top. As she washed her hands, she noticed the paper was yellowed, like it was old, and curiosity overcame her.

She unfolded it, laying it out on the bench, ignoring the kitten, who was making some weird noises.

It was a faded poster from around the 1940's, she thought, from the lettering style and fashion. She moved her fingers away from the top corner where it was torn, like it had been pinned up and quickly pulled down. Placing it on the table, she unrolled it carefully. On it was a picture of a woman, dressed in a turquoise dress, singing on a stage. The words, 'The Bluejay' were in block letters above her head. Below, it said: 'Come and hear her and take your blues away. Friday 7th November'.

Esther smiled. It was beautiful and understated. The woman was young and looked up from heavily lidded eyes. She folded the poster up again and tucked it in behind the recipe books. That would fit in nicely on her bookshelves in a second hand frame.

A horrible noise, a mix of a yowl and squawk, came from the lounge and she ran in to see a bundle of kitten and bird tumbling towards the ground. How had she forgotten about Louis?

The bird squawked, but the kitten had a good grip on it.

Esther ran over. "Stop. No!"

The bird was awake now, and managed to get itself free and stand up, while the kitten shook its tiny rump, prepared for another pounce. The bird took off and flew unsteadily towards the back of the couch, then changed direction to stop at the top of the shelves, feathers ruffled and chest moving in and out.

Esther scooped the kitten up underneath its tummy, before it decided to try and scale Mt Bookshelves, in search of its prey, and locked it in her room.

She sat down to watch the television. The bird fluttered down and alighted on the floor. Then she lifted the heavy window up.

"Off you go," she said. "Go on, be free."

The bird tilted its head forward and lifted its wings.

"What's the matter?" she asked, as it hopped sideways away from the window. "Are you scared of that silly kitty? Are you hungry?"

The bird fluttered up to the bookshelves again, leaving a white mess on the floor.

"Ooh," she growled. "You need a bit of training, don't you?" She grabbed some paper towels and bent down to wipe it up.

It flew over her and out the window, then, and Esther felt something inside her sink.

Phoebe called that night, as Esther was relaxing on the couch.

"How are you going, Esther? Do you still want any information about *that* Friday evening?"

"Yes, of course. I am apparently an investigator now," she said, sarcastically. "Do you remember anything else from that last shift?"

"Well, I have remembered something. But the more I think about it, the more I'm not sure if I remember correctly. Everyone was shoving out the door, but I never actually saw Jayden leave." Phoebe said.

"But you went in to do the cleaning?"

"Yeah, I started vacuuming. I did actually check around. I turn all the lights on, otherwise it can be very dark in the corners. Didn't see anyone."

"And the back door was shut?"

"Yeah, it locks on shutting," Phoebe said. "I did have my headphones on, so I wouldn't have heard anything."

Esther thought about what she knew about Jayden, and realized that it was pretty much nothing. It was amazing how you could work with someone for a couple of years, even if it was only a day a fortnight, and know next to nothing about them. It was usually Ashton and Jo that she talked to.

"What do you think he was doing?"

"I don't want to say anything bad about him..." Phoebe leaned close. "But maybe he was doing something sneaky. Stealing money?"

"No, I very much doubt that."

"He is always complaining about money, though. And coming up with schemes. And talking about how much his wife's hair extensions cost."

"Yeah, but..." She thought it through. "The takings were already gone, and the float was with Rochelle."

"What if there was something else worth taking in the shop? In Rochelle's office?"

"You've been watching too many crime shows, I think," she laughed.

"It's lucky one of us has," Phoebe said, as if this was the exact situation that she had been waiting for, and now she was going to come into her own. Perhaps she did have a point, but something niggled at Esther's mind about the timing. Phoebe came in and started vacuuming, about 5:30. Everyone else had just left.

"Did you do anything else when you first came in?"

"No, I literally put down my bag and went straight to get the vacuum out..."

Esther looked at her. "Where is the vacuum kept?"

"In that little cupboard room thing off the back room."

"So you would have had to turn your back on the door for a minute or so?"

Phoebe lifted her eyes, and shivered. "Do you think..."

Esther leaned over and patted her shoulder. "Well, we know that Rochelle went back towards the shop after she left me. You said you think you didn't see Jayden leave. So... what if he hid somewhere, then snuck out past you and they met outside?"

"But why?"

Phoebe lifted her eyebrows pointedly. "An affair," she said. "A crime of passion."

"I mean, it is possible," she said, doubtfully.

How was she going to check this out? Esther wasn't sure, so she decided to ask Rochelle's husband. It wouldn't be pretty and she felt guilty doing it but it was a logical next step, short of being able to go through Rochelle's cell phone, or questioning Jayden, she didn't know what else to do.

"Night, Phoebe," she said. *That* was a problem for tomorrow. Right now, she had a date with her bed, her kitten and a book.

"I don't know anything else. I've said it all 100 times. Are you a journalist or something?"

Greg slammed the bag down on the bench, and Esther cringed. He almost seemed like he had two different personalities. Why had she come alone?

"No," she said and pulled out an object from her bag. "I just want us not to have to be afraid anymore. It's been a lot more difficult than I thought it would have been."

"Too bloody right," he said. "Nothing's black and white. Now make it quick, I've got to take my dog to the vet."

Esther felt that nothing was black and white was more profound than any eulogy. "I don't want to upset you... again. I really don't, but I've got a good lead on what might have happened. Is there any possibility at all that she was... carrying on with somebody else? Any chance?"

At this point, she was quite certain that she must have a death wish herself. The silence stretched on.

"No," he said. "Of course not." He stood up.

"I didn't really think so," she put in quickly.

"Yes you did. Because she was a glorious angel and I… I'm a grease monkey factory worker. But do you know why I know that it's not true? Do you?"

She shook her head.

"I know, without a doubt, that she'd tell me. You're too young to know about marriages. But we're both on our second round. She'd break up with me straight away." He clapped himself on the chest. "We had talked about it, so I know all her thoughts on the matter. She wouldn't have worried about hurting me. She could be quite blunt now and then, I don't know if you noticed."

"Hm," she said.

"Not a chance in hell." Greg grinned but he had two burning red patches in his cheeks. "Now, I've got to get going."

Esther had to admit he was very convincing. But now she wasn't entirely convinced that Greg shouldn't be the prime suspect. Then again, maybe he was right to be that angry. She glanced back at the house as she drove off, and he was still watching from the step.

CHAPTER 14

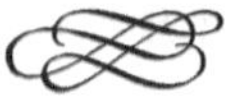

"I had to get you back again, dear," her nan said, when Esther arrived at the rest home. "I didn't explain things very well yesterday. It might be better if I show you, actually."

"Okay…"

"Well—" Her nan mimed holding a microphone, and tilted her head slightly. "They called me the Bluejay. Not that jays are any great singers, but they have a great range with their voice."

Esther saw the years drop away suddenly, and remembered her nan's powerful voice from when she had sung in the rest home recreation room.

"That's you? Why didn't you tell me?" Esther asked her nan. It all would have been much simpler if people would just communicate. Why did it all have to be so secretive?

"Hang on, have you heard of me? Have you heard that name?"

"I've got a poster. It came from… well, I'm not sure, really."

Her nan looked at her sadly. "I couldn't tell you. Your mother made me promise. Well, no, it's stronger than a promise really, more like a vow."

Her mother? "But why would she do that?"

"I interfered. When you were very young, I got involved in something. Your mother bound me to a vow that I wouldn't tell you any of it."

"Nothing? Hang on."

"She grew up just with me, as you know. We moved to a little town where nobody knew us, and I struggled so hard. It was bleeding tough in those days, love— I'd just lost your grandfather, and people were funny about us living together and being happy without anyone else to look after us. I was singing at nights, and I'd take her along. I know it wasn't the best place for a little one but she got along pretty well. But people talked, as they do. It must have seemed odd, a single mother and daughter with a beautiful house and car. A few said things about us, awful things, that I was selling my body or getting paid as an escort. I just let them talk, but I'm afraid your mum must have suffered at school.

Anyway, she got married to your dad and life happened, as it tends to. Then when you and your brother came along, I wanted to help you out. I gave your parents bits of money for things, like baby cots and music lessons. But I'm afraid I overstepped the line one day when I came to your school."

There was a knock at the door and it opened inwards. "Come on, Hope, it's time for housie." The man who had wanted his dinner during her song stuck his face around the door.

"I'm with my granddaughter at the moment, Kevin," her nan said.

"Oh." The door closed again.

Her nan shook her head. "Perhaps we should go and sit outside in the grounds?"

"Yes, good idea," she said.

When they were seated on the bench seat outside, with a blanket looped around their shoulders, her nan continued.

"You know, I love to sing, but of course it was much harder when your mother was born," she said. She ran her fingers over the back of the park bench, her eyes far away. "From the very first time I sang in church and brought tears to the eyes of the parish. Well, one of the men asked me to sing at a club. I was just a girl, really. I was only 16 and shy as anything."

Esther raised her eyebrows, thinking it must have been scandalous.

"It was thought a little odd," her nan conceded, "but

that first time was only in the afternoon, and the amount I was paid obviously made it worth it for my father. It was all long ago. Another life, really." She waved her hand as if that was of no consequence now. "There was a boy in the audience that first night — he told me that I showed him what dreams sound like. I was just a farm girl before that. I was flattered but I thought he was silly and idealistic."

"The club owner was happy so I kept on singing and the audience kept on coming. And one night the boy bought me a drink and he told me that my voice made it feel like summer. 'Do you know what I do in summer? ' he asked. 'I laugh a lot and I dance'. He looked so happy.

One night, when I went to the club, the air felt out-of-balance somehow. I had this spiky feeling that something bad had happened. Anyway, I still got on the stage, and as I sang, the harmonies and melodies came into tune and all sounded right to me.

"No one said anything that night, but the whispers around the town said that Joseph Matthews was—" She paused. "I'm going to have to stop there. My tongue feels a little fuzzy. Like numb."

"Are you alright?"

"Anyway, I just did what I liked," she continued on. "One night, the boy and I started kissing and just never stopped. Inevitably, my courses stopped and my belly just kept swelling and swelling.

My parents, especially my father, acted like I was invisible, even though I was literally hard to miss, so I just kept singing until I couldn't anymore. I tried bringing the baby along with me for a while..." She stopped.

Esther put her hand over her Grandma's soft skin and they sat there together as the lights changed to greys and purples, touched with gold. Birds twittered and called to each other. She felt a deep satisfaction, knowing that she was a part of something greater, a magical family. It was an ordinary sort of magic, one for those that listened and waited.

"I'm proud of you," Esther said quietly. She didn't think anyone had said that to her nan before. "But why couldn't you tell me any of that?"

Her nan just shook her head.

Esther knew what happened next. The boy had left. They had moved to another town, just her and the baby.

"Nan? Come back in, it's too cold for you out here."

It was the first time that her nan hadn't had some witty argument. She must be almost frozen solid, Esther thought.

In all the excitement, she had forgotten to get presents for her family. Her brothers, Aaron and Brad, would be happy with a gift voucher. Her other brother, Phillip, would probably want a video game. So that just left her mum and dad.

She stopped in at the pharmacy, drawn to a gorgeous window display, with jewellery dripping from wire Christmas trees, and scarves in luscious fabrics of mustard, rust, burgundy and forest green.

Her mum usually bought herself whatever she needed; the latest navy and grey clothes from the catalogue. Perhaps she'd like one of those foot care gift bags? She groaned. Who was she kidding? Her mum would never use that. She didn't stay still long enough.

Everyone called it the pharmacy, but it was done up

like an old-fashioned apothecary, with jars and hand-written labels. Esther supposed it was for the tourists, mostly, but she loved the shop. She crossed the threshold, ducking her head under hanging strings of garlic and bunches of herbs.

"No, you can do it yourself!" Well, that was a familiar voice. Clark. She couldn't see him in the shop. He must be out the back.

Esther pretended to browse the shelves, while listening as hard as she could. She picked things up at random and put them down again. She opened a tube and sniffed the vanilla scent.

Clark stomped out of the back room, turning his head to look at her. Just then, one of the assistants came over, eyeing the products on the shelf in front of her. "Can I help you with... fungal cream?"

"Oh, no, thanks." she said, turning away, face burning.

Clark turned and grinned at her, and she stalked past to get out of the shop. In her frustration, she pushed where the door clearly said pull and almost got hit in the face.

He followed her out. "Are you alright?"

"Of course I am," she snapped, speeding up. "I'm going to my car."

He caught up with her and reached out as if to grab her arm. "Wait a minute," he said. "I was just going to say that you didn't pay for that hand cream. Leah called out to you as you left."

Esther turned around and looked down at the exquisite scrolls and golden embossing on the label. Oh, Goodness. She was only holding a fifty pound tube of moisturiser in her hand.

"Shit." As she realized that she had just burgled a shop right in front of a police officer, her whole body went white hot, from her legs to the top of her head. She thought she might vomit.

"It's… " But he trailed off. "Are you okay?"

She walked over to the side a few steps, to try and get some air but black spots pressed in on the edges of her vision, and she found it hard to catch her breath. *Oh no,* she thought. *Not now. Not now. Not now not now—*

Then a warm hand squeezed her shoulder. "It's alright, I can see it was just a mistake," he said.

"Thanks," she said, head hanging down between her knees.

She straightened up slowly, and he put his hand on her shoulder. "I've had some training, you know, for my job. Come on, I'll take you for a cup of tea," he said, pointing to the tea rooms.

"No, I don't have time." She shook her head.

"Oh, go on. Just wait here one minute and I'll take this back in." He jogged into the pharmacy.

They sat at a little table and he ordered them a pot of tea.

"Close your eyes."

She narrowed her eyes but she had to admit she was feeling better just sitting down. Was this some sort of interrogation technique?

He gestured to her to go ahead. "Go on. Shut them."

She shut them, feeling absurdly vulnerable and still on the edge of a panic attack. She thought for a moment that he was going to kiss her, and wondered what that would feel like, then pushed the thought away. That was just crazy. He was a cop. He didn't bring her here for that. It was just to avoid a scene in the carpark.

"I once went on holiday to this island, and it was so beautiful it hurt to look at. We walked along the lower fortifications of a white stone citadel to get to the beach. It was lined with tables and colourful umbrellas and I could smell pizza cooking and huge slabs of rotisserie meat slowly turned on sticks. Some of the street food vendors called out, pointing to their special of the day."

His voice was even and calm, and she couldn't help but be drawn in.

"People were relaxed, laughing. Someone on the beach was carrying three scoops of gelato in a cone. I sat in the fine white sand, drinking an icy cold cola and watched the sunlight glinting off the sea. When I went in the water, it was crystal clear. I floated in the sea, on my back, and all sound faded away until only the cool on my skin, the smell of salt and the heat of the sun above remained. It was the most peaceful I've felt."

She opened her eyes to see him watching her. "Why did you tell me all of that?"

He smiled. "I could see that you were anxious."

"Some sort of cop trick?" She didn't mean it to come out so sarcastic, but he was a little unpredictable. The waitress brought over her pot of tea and a little jug of milk.

"Something like that. It was all true, though."

"Okay." The warmth of the tea rooms was starting to relax her shoulders.

"When you try your tea, notice the flavours, the temperature. Try to notice something about the cup. Does it have any chips, any discolouration. Is there a drop in the saucer?"

She poured out her tea, and picked up the cup, turning it to examine it for any discolourations.

"Notice your heart beat and your breathing. Has it slowed?"

"A little," she said, although it started speeding up again as he began rolling up the sleeves of his shirt, drawing attention to his shapely forearms. "What do you like doing?" she asked, to take the attention away from her vitals.

"It's been a long time since I've done anything for myself. My job is pretty demanding."

After a pause, she said, "I suppose it would be." She wished he'd open up about himself a bit more and wondered if they had anything in common at all. "You must get some downtime, though. What's your favourite thing to watch?"

"I don't watch a lot of telly. I do like movies though... Top Gun, Police Academy..."

Esther tried to stop herself from making a face. "Uh huh, yep."

"And musicals like Bohemian Rhapsody, Walk the Line, Once... "

She leaned forward. "Alright, now we're talking. Once is so great. I saw the show when it came."

"So did I."

She sang a few notes from the main song.

"That's it," he said. "You're a great singer. My kiddo— "

Esther felt her mouth drop open. "Ah... "

"She's my sister, really. Triss. She wanted to go, but I ended up enjoying it more than her."

"Is it really hot in here?" she asked.

"Yeah, it is," he replied, looking at the windows, which seemed to be painted shut. He lowered his voice. "We should talk a bit about where we're at with the case. I found out something disturbing about the cleaner."

"Phoebe?"

"She told us that the victim didn't come back to the shop, but we know she did. Her alibi was her mother, who said Phoebe got home at around 6:00. After having been to the supermarket. So Phoebe doesn't know if Rochelle came back to the shop, as she wasn't there," he finished, triumphantly.

"She didn't do the cleaning?"

"Not for very long, at any rate." Clark looked down at his phone which was buzzing. He answered, and said he had to go.

"Alright, thanks," Esther said. Phoebe had lied to her. She could see why she had felt the need to. She wanted to get paid for her full shift.

"I'll see you again soon," he said, in his very direct way. It sounded as if he was already looking forward to it.

"Bye," she said, and waved, cursing how flirty her voice sounded.

She dialled Aria, and immediately regretted it, when she laughed for a full minute. When she caught her breath, Aria said, "Sorry, you went to a quilting club? You?"

"Yes," she said, rolling her eyes.

"I'm surprised they let you in."

"They were very welcoming, actually."

"Cheer up, Essie, wouldn't you rather your friends laugh at you than your enemies?"

"I suppose so."

"Okay, I've got some news to report back. So Troy talked to your mate Jayden after their Body Smash class the other day. Apparently, he doesn't love working at the bookshop. Like, dealing with the customers and all that. It's just something to do while he waits to strike it rich. He did say that he really respects Rochelle though. She's taken the bookshop from a stuffy, rundown hole to a cosy, fun shop filled with books and toys."

"Oh, that's nice."

"Then he said he was sponsored to go to a theme park last weekend with his wife. He's just hit a new subscriber goal because he filmed some spoilt kids having tantrums in the line."

Esther sighed. That sounded about right. Jayden was always boasting about his prowess with social media. "My wife and I met on a hashtag," was one of the first things he said to her, and she still found it a bizarre thing to say.

"We were both posting on Insta under #hotsidehustles. Mine was photography and hers was selling scent burners. We both recognized each other's ambition straight away."

"He sounds like a real winner," Aria said.

"Okay, yeah, I admit he is a bit... odd, but that's not enough reason for him to be a suspect."

"Listen to you, you sound so professional!"

One step forward, and two steps back. She was tempted to have a tantrum herself.

CHAPTER 16

$\mathcal{A}$ memory came back to her, sudden and vivid, from when she was eleven. Esther was stretched out on her stomach in a sunny patch on the floor in the lounge, twirling her headband in one hand. She couldn't hear her own thoughts for the banging on the piano. Her brother's friend Tina was using their instrument to practise on.

The homework assignment was due tomorrow, but Esther had started daydreaming. What if the RMS Titanic had never sunk? If it had continued its beautiful journey onwards through the North Atlantic, and all those people named in print were still alive, instead of just a number? Her mind followed the life path of the passengers. What if all those in third class had all had children, and their children had had children?

Tina clunked her way through a scale. Esther pressed her lead into the paper and it broke. She put her thumb on the top of the pencil and the lead moved down. Her brother had gone out to the park and she was left with the terrible noise.

She grabbed an apple from the bowl and crunched into it, eyeing Tina from the kitchen. Now Tina was playing a note on the piano and opening her mouth. Esther guessed she was trying to match the note. It sounded to her like what she supposed a cake would taste like, if you dropped egg shells in it. It would start off fine, then you'd crunch into something and you'd be picking it out of your teeth for ages afterwards.

Esther looked out the window. She knew a few songs that her nan had taught her when she came over, but her mum said she wouldn't pay for piano lessons until Esther was older. She didn't think this was fair, because Phil had lessons when he was twelve, and he never even practised, then just gave up.

Tina played a note and held it for one, two, three. Esther saw the note in her mind; a round, purple thing floating through the air, not quite finished. She opened her mouth and completed it.

She turned around and saw Tina staring at her. Heat ran up her face as she realized she'd sung it out loud.

"I just sung—"

"No, look at this," Tina cried, and stumbled back from the piano. "Look!"

Esther walked towards the instrument. She could see the keys moving up and down, although Tina was now back against the wall.

Esther herself wasn't afraid and lifted the lid of the piano to see what was happening. She normally loved to watch the little hammers hit the strings.

As she lifted the heavy lid, she felt something cool brush past the hairs on her arms. The keys had stopped moving. She let the lid down with a sonorous sound.

"It seems to have stopped," she said.

"But I saw it," Tina gabbled, tears streaming down her face. "There. Out the window. A man with a suitcase in old-fashioned clothes," she said.

It was one of those rare afternoons when her mother was at home, and she came through from the study now and stood in the doorway.

"What's happening? Tina, are you alright?"

Tina scrabbled to her feet, rubbed at her eyes, and stopped in the doorway. She pointed at Esther.

"She made it! She did it!"

Although her mother asked her about it, Esther couldn't explain what happened.

"We will just forget about it, and she will eventually too," her mother said.

Tina never came back to the house, although her

parents tried to bring her back a couple of times. Esther guessed they must have paid for a whole term of lessons in advance. Tina shook her head, face stuck in a stubborn frown and her parents eventually gave up, apologising profusely. It didn't stop her spreading around school that the Forte house was haunted.

Music had always been there, guiding and coaching her, growing and supporting her. When she had trouble getting to sleep, music helped her. When the struggles slapped her down, music caressed her and gently stood her on her feet, and nudged her to keep walking.

This was one of those times when she thought the music wasn't on her side at all. It made things happen, but not good things. Sometimes it betrayed her.

The memory left her gasping. It was so vivid. How had she pushed that so far down that she had mostly forgotten it?

CHAPTER 17

"*J*knew you'd come to it in your own time," her nan said, eyes sparkling. They were sitting in her room and the winter sun shone thinly through the gaps in the blinds.

Esther got up to look out the window. The trees below waved their branches in the wind and the grass rippled. In the distance, she could see the green of Flat Rock Reserve. "Come to what?"

"The craft," she said. "It just took you a little bit longer. Like learning to ride your bike when you were a wee girl. Sometimes you get there in your own good time."

"Yeah, I'm like a cheese," she said, wryly.

Her nan laughed. "Don't be hard on yourself, dear."

"So, what is the craft? Sounds very mysterious."

"Well, I'm not sure if I can tell you, but I'll try." Her nan looked behind her, although there was no one else nearby.

Esther was wearing a long woollen cardigan and she wrapped it around herself now, as a chill passed through her. "What's going to happen?" she asked, flippantly.

"Well, I'm a witch." Her nan picked up a biscuit and crunched into it, eyes half closed in bliss.

"I figured that out already."

"Alright, smarty pants." Her nan swallowed her mouthful. "We don't know that much about it, because people in my day never talked about things, you know. My parents were frightfully angry if I mentioned anything, so we assume it started with me. Your mum definitely is one, and probably your brother too."

Esther was about to ask which brother, but swallowed the question. It was obviously Philip. It had to be.

"Music is in our blood, literally, but it works a little differently depending on who it is. I seem to be able to heal people from whatever it is that ails them, from depression to stopping smoking to gout and quinsy."

Quinsy? "What is... oh, never mind." She waved her hand.

"I had to work by trial and error some of the time. Your mother used to help me when she was little. I'd doodle songs everywhere and test them out without people knowing. Sometimes they failed. Sometimes they worked."

"It sounds very random."

"I did little healing spells on my family and myself from time to time." Her nan stood up and reached for a framed photo on the shelf. Not for the first time, Esther wondered about how well-preserved her grandmother was, for her ninety odd years. Perhaps she had figured out a little anti-ageing spell.

"Your mother used to be a very accomplished witch." Her nan raised her eyebrows at her, as if Esther wouldn't believe that. But she sighed to herself. That was the problem. Her mother was a little too perfect at everything.

"Paula could help people make a decision without emotion. People used to come round and ask her for help. The magic turned out to be very useful in her line of work. She used to sing to herself in break times to make sure she could be objective in her work. I'm not sure if she still does though."

Ester tried to imagine her mother as a young judge wanting to be taken seriously. It would have been difficult being a woman in that job, and to have secretly been a witch in that position as well. Did she really sing to herself to get rid of the emotion so she could make a balanced decision?

Yes, the answer came to her. She remembered the night when a young Esther had listened from the top of the stairs, and one of her mother's friends had come, asking for her mother's help, for the strength to make a hard decision.

And how many other decisions had her mother made that way? Decisions about Esther's life? Sending nan away to a rest home in another town? Pushing the boys towards Accounting? Spending more time at her tennis club than at home?

"Your brother is just getting to grips with his own unique style," her nan said. "I think he'll understand more in the next couple of years."

But Esther was already onto the next thing. "What do you think I'll be able to do? I'm pretty sure I brought some frogs out of the ground the other day."

"Frogs, you say?" With a wave of her hand, she dismissed the rogue amphibians, but leaned forward. "The real question is, why now?"

"I'm not sure," she said. "Oh yes, do you know of the quilting club here in town?"

"Yes, I know Moran and Joanie. Have they been trying to recruit you?"

"Sort of."

"They do need some young ones to take up the mantle, so to speak."

"I'm not sure how many young people are into quilting, though."

"Yes, that is an issue. Do you know what we need

when discussing this? A little spot of tea. Would you like to find Brenda to bring us a pot? Or pop along to the kitchenette and make it yourself?"

"Yeah, sure." Esther shut the door and headed down the long hallway to the nurses station. She couldn't see anyone in there, so she kept going to the room marked 'Kitchen'. It was only the size of a walk-in wardrobe, really, and there was a man in there, whistling to himself. By the time she had waited through two rounds of 'Jingle Bell Rock', Esther was gritting her teeth as she poured the hot water into the teapot. She set two cups on the tray and picked it up. She was only halfway down the long hallway when she heard her nan's raised voice, strong and charismatic. Was she singing?

She rushed back in, to find the door wide open and Hope's hair messy. Her nan was standing in the middle of the room.

"Are you alright?" Esther looked around for somewhere to put the tray down and clanked it down rather harder than she meant to. Her nerves were jangling with adrenalin. She hugged her nan tight.

"There was a fellow. He tried to lock me in here. But I got rid of him," she said, proudly.

"What? What did you do to him?" Esther asked, genuinely curious if she had perhaps turned him into a toad.

"Oh, nothing," she said, "but when he saw how powerful I was, he turned and ran."

"You sung at him?"

"Lucky you weren't in the room, dear, or I wouldn't have been able to," she said with a bitter laugh. "Dratted vow."

Esther hugged her nan tight again, more for her own benefit than Hope's. She was about to tell her to be careful, then realised that she really didn't need to. Her nan was much better equipped to defend herself than she was.

"Come to my place. It's around this corner." She'd called Clark right after the incident at the rest home. He met her at the bookshop. Her hands were still shaking and she felt a little short of breath. What if her nan had been asleep or unable to sing? What if Esther had been coming through the door? Suddenly, the mystery was much more urgent.

"Righto."

"She said it was a man, but she didn't get a good look at him. I suppose he could have been working for whoever it is." She brushed away the sudden thought that it could have been Esther he was after. No, he had specifically waited until she left the room.

"Hmm. And he just ran off?"

She opened the door to her flat, acutely aware of his

presence next to her. Ever since they met, she had been continually embarrassing herself around him. She wasn't used to feeling like that. She unlocked the door, briefly wondering if she had left it messy.

It looked fine, but she went through to the kitchen to flick on the jug.

"Ah, who's this little kitty?"

"Don't—" Too late, she turned around to see him reaching down towards the ground.

Louis was lying on his back, fluffy silver tummy exposed. One of Clark's deliciously juicy looking hands was descending towards the trap. One second of delightful tickling ensued, as she watched in horror.

"Ah, sh—" He jerked his hand away.

"Are you ok? I'm so sorry."

"Yeah I'm—" he started to say.

"No, you're bleeding." A line of red dots had appeared on his palm, and welled into thick red drops.

"Oh that little bas—"

She cringed. "That should really be his name at this point. You sit down, I'll go get something for it."

She rummaged in the medical supplies drawer, throwing old prescription pills and nose sprays out of the way.

"Can I have your hand — I mean, see your hand?" He put his hand out and she stuck the plaster over the cut, wrapping it around the edge of his finger. She looked up and his eyes were burning into her. He looked as if he was about to say something but she moved away.

After sending the kitten away sternly, she pulled down a teapot and made some tea. Food was what they needed. She looked in the cupboard, feeling uninspired. Would he like a cupcake or a biscuit?

Wow, as if it matters, she thought to herself. He was the policeman in charge of the case, and it was all sorts of wrong to get involved with him.

Her phone rang, and Phoebe's quiet voice said hello. "I just wanted to give you an update on the funeral. I talked to Greg a little about where he was that weekend. Rochelle's sister was staying with them and said he never left, and that's why the police haven't suspected him. He was happy enough to talk about it."

"Thanks," she said. "He's an odd one, that one."

"You won't guess who that was," she said, stopping in the doorway to the lounge. She looked up and the bloody bird was perched on his shoulder. Esther narrowed her eyes. She could have sworn it saw her looking, turned its head and nibbled at his earlobe.

He put his hand up to it gingerly.

"Do you like birds then?" she asked.

"Seems I do." He seemed calm enough, but his eyes flicked upwards when it fluttered up onto his head. "And they like me more than cats do."

She smiled and sat down. "I'm sorry about the bird.

He just sort of appeared one day. Just wave your hand around and he'll fly off."

"How does it work with the cat and bird living together?"

"Oh, it doesn't. At all." She laughed. "But they have both adopted me, and I can't really kick them out now."

"I suppose not." He was bending his head forward, so as not to annoy the bird. Its head came forward and it lifted its wings. Esther was getting more and more nervous, but Clark seemed happy enough for the moment.

"Ok, so, where are we at?" She pulled out her laptop. "I've got the spreadsheet here. This column is for reasons why it could be them. This one is for reasons against. She stopped talking. He was staring at her.

"You're pretty good at this."

She could just see his eyes through his glasses.

"So what do we need to think about next? Motive?"

"Greg's motive could be the life insurance payout. And he could be working with Rochelle's sister."

"No, I doubt that. What do you think about Vicky?"

"What about her?" Esther stared into the distance. Although Vicky did have the most to gain, she didn't seem the type to meticulously plan a murder. She couldn't even plan a lunch.

"Well, you told me that Vicky planned to meet with Rochelle on Saturday morning."

She let her eyes drift over his face, lingering on his lips. "I've got this thing to go to tomorrow night. Do you want to come with me?" Esther kicked herself. Why had she asked him like that?

"Well…"

"It's my friend's engagement party. On at the town hall. And, well, you could come along, just to check everyone out. Not like a date or anything. I mean, I'm not sure how safe I feel. After what happened to Nan."

He took his glasses off and wiped them with the hem of his jersey. His eyes were burning into her intensely.

"I was about to say I'd love to come. Does he have a name?"

"Who? Oh, um, I call him 'Bird', among other things."

"What about Jay? That's what he is, I think."

She felt herself drawn towards him, imagining how soft his lips would be. She could tell he would be a great kisser.

Then it happened. Something white appeared on the front of his shirt. The bird bobbed its head, ever so slightly.

"What. Ugh!"

"Don't move," she said. The mess was very close to the neckline of his shirt.

She flapped her hand at the bird and it flew up to the bookshelves. She carefully pulled the shirt over his head.

"I'll rinse this off and put it in the machine. Have you got anything else to wear?"

"I've got my jersey."

Before she turned away, she couldn't help but notice he was slightly built, but with the hint of muscle in his shoulders. But what caught her eye was the sleeve tattoo — a leopard with one half of its face stripped back to the bone.

"Or should I just keep it off?" he asked, as she walked through into the kitchen, a hint of mocking in his voice.

"Please yourself," she said, although she longed to trace that tattoo with her fingers. A sudden image came into her head of his warm skin, and the crisp, clean linen of bed sheets. "It wouldn't be professional of me to even notice."

"Uh huh."

Was she flirting again?

"I don't date policemen."

What a contradiction he was. On the outside, he was gentle and very considered about everything. But a tattoo meant he had an impulsive side. Although, he might have considered the design for five years before taking the plunge. She longed to ask him.

When she came back in, he was wearing his jersey.

"Alright, so I don't think it's Raid. What do you think?"

"He was in the right place at the right time."

"What's his motive?"

"Well, I can formulate a theory. But it would be based on…"

She burst out laughing. "You're the worst cop I've ever seen."

The clock in the shelves ticked in the silence. Clark fiddled with his sleeve, obviously wrestling with something. He heaved a sigh.

"Sorry, I didn't mean—"

"Honesty is really important to me. Especially with people I care about."

"Of course. Your job—

"That's because I'm not," he said. "A policeman. My name *is* Aiden Clark. But my surname is Thomas. I'm a Professor of Parapsychology at the University of Edinburgh."

"Wait, what? So the policeman looking after Rochelle's case is not a policeman at all?" Esther stood up, and heat rose up her body and into her cheeks. "You are a professor?"

"Yes," he said, calmly. "I was sent here for a year to investigate paranormal phenomena. Sort of a secondment. There are a lot of strange happenings in this town."

Esther kept her voice calm. "Like what?"

"Oh, mostly Extra Sensory Perception, you know, ESP, whether dreams can predict reality, out-of-body experiences, psychokinesis. Well, really micropsychokinesis, to be more accurate. It's an interesting field."

"I'm sure it is." Esther put her hands on her hips. "So how much of what I know about you was real?"

He reached forward and pulled her in, until she was standing right in front of him. Her traitorous body zinged.

"This," he said, looking up at her. "The time you and I have spent together was real. I feel like I know you, Esther. You work in a music store. You've got a great bunch of friends and you're so loyal. You can draw like anything. I can't wait to hear you sing. You're really brave."

"Am I?" She pulled away. Should she be worried that he had lied to her? He was undercover so he had no choice.

And what had she done? She hadn't exactly been upfront with him about the whole magical thing. But to be fair, she didn't know what exactly was going on there herself.

"You live with anxiety every day, yet you get up and get going. You talk to people. You're even doing a better job with the case than the coppers."

"So you don't have your sister living with you?"

"I promise you that Triss is real. She's eleven and I've been her guardian since she was eight. She's noisy and enthusiastic and really smart. I can't wait for you to meet her." He smiled and it changed his whole face. A warm feeling spread around her insides.

She leaned her face down but stopped just a few centimetres from his face. "And did you holiday down at the lake when you were a child?"

"Yes, I did. That part was real, too."

"I knew you were lying about not wanting to be a detective."

"Well, I didn't want to be a detective, so that part was true. I'm sorry, alright. I'm telling you everything right now."

He pulled her close, and she gave in to the hug, her whole body tingling with wanting to be close to him.

"Please," he said into her hair. "You have nothing to worry about, because I'm not really a policeman. Just a professor far from home."

CHAPTER 19

*E*sther was baking again, this time it was chocolate chip cookies. *I'll probably eat them all by the end of the weekend, too,* she thought.

She pulled off a little of the cookie dough, and savoured the buttery taste. Now that she had some distance from the fuzz of attraction, she reflected on Clark again.

If he was here to investigate paranormal activity, perhaps he had seen the incident with the frogs and knew that she was magical. Perhaps he wanted to take her back to his lab and perform experiments on her. She thought back, but he hadn't seemed to be too suspicious of her. Only Ashton.

Still, she thought it wouldn't do to let slip about her new abilities. If you could call them that.

He's a good actor, a little voice told her. *He's been acting this whole time and you didn't know.*

"I had some idea that he wasn't a great policeman," she burst out. The jay flew off the couch with a squawk and flutter of feathers and landed on top of the bookshelves.

Louis puffed up his fur and stretched out his claws.

He's definitely doing his best to make you feel comfortable with him.

Perhaps he was being a genuine person. And he knew that she had anxiety.

She flicked on the television and looked for any musicals. A documentary about the Titanic came on, and she settled in. She used to be obsessed with the Titanic. Louis climbed over her and found a good spot in the crook of her leg, which meant she couldn't move now, even if she wanted to.

She fiddled with her phone, then made up her mind. She rang through to Clark. "Where were you on that Friday?" she asked.

There was a silence that stretched.

"Don't do this, Esther," he said. "Of course I can tell you where I was. I was with Shona and we were looking into a case. You can ask her."

"Alright, I'm sorry. It is really tough when you're questioning everything and everyone."

"I know. Believe me," he said. "But don't you think Shona would have me in cuffs, already, if she suspected?"

"She would too."

Esther was thoroughly perplexed with the mystery, but she had one lead left to follow. A weak one, for sure. She had to head to the source of all gossip in the town. As she crossed the moonlit road, she checked left and right. Ledstow was quiet and the tips of her fingers tingled with cold.

It was freezing in the café as one of the windows was open, and Esther chose a spot on the opposite side to sit down between Moran and Lottie, her back to the fire.

"You're just in time, love."

As they joined the squares together, they spoke a few low words that Esther couldn't catch.

Esther realized that the picture on the quilt was a representation of Ledstow, with the red and white triangles representing the hills, cream and brown squares for the new housing, the snaky ribboning river. There was the dark green for the woods, the silver lake, and there, the church and graveyard.

"That's amazing," she breathed.

A sweet, incense smell filled the air, and faint purple shimmering lights rose up from the seams, almost like those pictures of the aurora. She couldn't tear her eyes from the dancing lights.

Something reset. Esther wasn't sure exactly what, but as her nan would say, she 'felt it in her waters'. The warm feeling in the top of her spine brought her closer to the people in the room, and she wanted to spill all her secrets to them and find out theirs.

Lottie stood up. "There," she said. "That's done for another month. Who's hungry?"

"You know I always am," Moran said, but he was looking right at Esther with a twinkle in his eye.

She followed Lottie out of the room, and waited until she opened the big fridge door out the back.

"Come on, Lottie. What are you really doing here? Will you give me a straight answer?" Esther watched Lottie's back stiffen, so she pressed further. "What was that? I felt something strange."

Lottie shut the fridge door with her back and leaned against it, a tray of cake in her hands.

"You want the truth? That was the protection ceremony we do each full moon."

"Alright," she said, slowly. These past weeks had taught her that more things were possible than she had considered. Sometimes, what people believed was their truth. "What are you protecting yourselves from?"

"Not us, love," she said, placing the tray on the bench and unwrapping the plastic. "You. All of you. Our beloved Ledstow. It's a bit of a haven. We've always wanted this place to be open to people, magical and not, who haven't got anywhere else to go. On the full moon, we sew protection and love into the town."

"Er, to protect it from what?"

"From anything. Any more questions?"

"How come you let *me* in while you were doing the spell, or ceremony, or whatever it is?"

Lottie rolled the plastic into a ball. "You're alright, Esther Forte. We can trust you," she said, simply. "Iris has been looking out for you. Did you know that she is Zany Grey herself? Keep that one quiet, though."

"Is she really?" How come every time she talked to Lottie she ended up with more questions than answers? It seemed to be a theme of her life at the moment.

"Anything else? I've got some hungry people out there."

"Just, thank you, I suppose."

Lottie's eyebrows lifted up. "You're welcome. How is it going with the cop?"

"What?"

"Nothing. Forget it."

Lottie looked as if she was about to burst out laughing. Esther grabbed the tea tray off the bench and went back into the other room, setting it on the table. "Sorry to disturb you all. But I don't suppose any of you check the community page?"

"I do look at it sometimes. How come, dear?"

"It's not that man complaining about his lawn getting trampled again, is it?" Moran said, grumpily.

"You'd think the school kids were digging up his grave, the way he carries on," Joanie added.

"No, I just wondered if any of you know of a Drew Donald who posts on there sometimes?"

"Hmm, that name rings a bell."

"You may be thinking of… Drew Donahue. He used to live here a long time ago, I think. Died of a heart attack," Joanie said.

Esther shrugged. "Can't be the same one then."

"I'd check out that cyclist if I were you," Moran said, patting her hand.

"What do you mean?"

"Oh, you know. Think about it," he said, tapping the side of his head.

"That's so rude," said Joanie. "We can't trust him to be polite to anyone younger than fifty, sorry. Thinks they're only half grown."

"I do not! I simply asked her to use her noggin."

"Hypocrit!"

Esther left quickly before they tried to get her involved in the argument, but later, it came to her with a sudden shock that the cyclist who had almost run her over that night may have something to do with the crime. Why hadn't she thought of that before?

CHAPTER 20

$\mathcal{C}$lark had called and said that the only person who was really into cycling was Vicky. He was busy at the police station so she asked Phoebe to accompany her to Vicky's house.

"Just as a witness, you know," she said. How terrible to think that way, but it was what she had to do now. This detective business made her suspicious of everybody.

She went up the path, pulse quickening with excitement. Was this it? Would Vicky say something to give herself away?

After a quick knock, the door pushed easily open. "Hello," she called, but all was quiet within.

She saw the edge of a shoe near the door and her heart skipped a beat as a vision of Vicky unconscious on the floor came into her mind. *Just a shoe*, she told herself, putting one hand to her heart, and breathed out in relief.

Phoebe poked her from behind. "What?" she mouthed.

Once the door was fully open, Esther could see piles of shoes and bags, almost as if somebody was packing. A sinking feeling gripped her as she walked inside. Where were the dogs?

A noise came from down the hall and they looked at each other. Phoebe's eyes were wide. They slipped off their shoes and crept down the hallway.

A noise that sounded like a faint sobbing was coming from the bedroom at the end. She called out again. But what she saw when she went in was not what she expected.

Vicky, who was always so well put together, was sitting at a table, hair messy, mascara streaks down her face. In front of her was a ouija board. She had a finger on a glass.

"What?" Vicky said, in an anguished voice. Esther took a step forward, but before she had opened her mouth, the woman continued.

"What should I do, my love?"

Glancing at Phoebe, whose face had paled, Esther chewed on her lip. There was something very intimate about the scene. Something that screamed 'do not disturb'.

As they watched, her finger and the cup began

moving across the board with a light scraping noise. It moved left and right, and Vicky's face remained the same, eyes closed. Esther wanted to see the board, but she felt frozen in place. Phoebe nudged her.

"People?" Vicky said in quite a different tone of voice. A shiver ran up Esther's spine and all the hairs on her body stood on end.

Vicky opened her eyes and turned toward them. She smacked her lips together a couple of times.

"I—"

"We are just going to go." Phoebe squeaked, and pulled on her sleeve.

"I don't think anyone has ever seen me talking to my husband in this way before. I can't believe I forgot to lock the door, but I've been in and out so often this morning."

"Your husband?" Esther blurted. It did feel like that sort of conversation between someone and their loved one, but Vicky's husband had died many years ago. He wasn't living anymore. Unless he was hiding out somewhere. Or she had a new one. Or something else.

Please have a new secret husband, she begged silently. *Please don't let it be communication from the other side.* But a small part of her, that had always been interested in the unexplained, was thrilled.

"Sorry, I must look dreadful." Vicky rubbed the skin beneath her eyes which only served to smudge her mascara even more.

"No," Phoebe lied. "You're fine." She turned to go again.

"I was just chatting to my love. You must think it's a pretty poor relationship, when he can only communicate by spelling things out. But really, it's enough, when it is all you've got."

Esther looked away, not wanting to meet Vicky's eyes.

"We really should leave." Phoebe said firmly.

"Communicate by spelling things out? Were you talking to him using the ouija board?"

For one moment, they all looked at each other. Esther was aware of everyone's breathing, her own and Phoebe's slightly fast breathing, and Vicky's ragged breath in. Perhaps there was something else there, too.

"Yes," she said. "In many ways, it's perfect. He's forever 44 and he gets to see me age and sag. It's not fair and it's not right."

"I'm sure…" Esther started, wanting to offer something, but platitudes didn't seem enough. "I don't think he would mind."

"I mind," she said, eyes flashing. "I can handle the lack of cuddles and not having a date at weddings. But I'd like to stay young."

"There's nothing you can do about it, though," she said. "We are all dying, but some more slowly than others."

"Then I'd like to make it the slowest possible," Vicky said, firmly.

"Just one quick thing. Have you been using an account in his name to post nasty comments on the community group?"

The look on her face changed from blank, to shock. She nodded. "It keeps him… alive for me."

"What was he telling you to do?" Esther asked, gently.

Clark arrived at the doorway, and Shona Norman arrived an instant later. Both of them in their full police uniforms were pretty intimidating, and Esther looked from Vicky to the policemen.

Clark winked at her, and a warm feeling spread through her.

"I didn't do it," Vicky said.

"Then why are you leaving?"

"My husband was telling me that you were going to come for me. He said you had evidence that it was me, and you wouldn't believe me. Is that what's happening? You believe me, don't you, Esther? Phoebe?"

CHAPTER 21

"A latté. Takeaway cup, thanks." Esther checked again that she had the decorations she needed in her bag.

Just then her friend burst into the shop. "Esther." Aria grabbed one of her hands in both of hers. "I've got a really bad feeling about tonight," she said.

"Why? Are you nervous?" She picked up her coffee and sat down at one of the tables.

Aria shook her head. "No, it should be super low-key. I just…"

Her friend often 'had a feeling' or dreamed about things before they happened. Esther was used to it. They usually laughed it off, but the way she worried at her lower lip now showed how stressed Aria was.

"I can't explain. Sorry."

"That's fine," she said. "Well, *I* have got a feeling that it's going to be great. Anything that happens, we can deal with it. And I'm bringing a plus one tonight," Esther said, trying to act casual. A little bit of distraction would be good for her friend. "I didn't think you'd mind."

Aria pounced on her as if she was the last chocolate bar in the house during her premenstrual week. "You're bringing someone along? As in, a date? Tell me everything."

She put her hands out in front in a placating way. "It's the policeman from the case, okay? Just there to help out."

"Is he going to be undercover at the party? That's so cool."

"I was worried you'd think he'd ruin it. It's just that I'm not feeling that safe."

"No, that is badass," Aria said, getting her lip gloss out of her bag. "I won't lie. It's a shame it's not someone you're interested in though, Esther. I want you to have someone who deserves you."

Clark maybe deserved her. He was worth a chance, anyway. She made herself say nothing, but her face must have given her away. It was the first time she had admitted to herself that going out with him was a possibility.

"What? You like him? But you can't date each other. He's a cop."

"Things may have changed a little," was all she said. Relationships were so complex, Esther thought.

"Ok, I do want to hear more. I'll just grab a coffee and I'll meet you next door."

They were just about to hang the last of the decorations in the old town hall, when Esther saw someone familiar walk in the front doors.

"Ash! How come they let you go?" She hugged him hard.

"They no longer have enough to hold me there. Maybe my Aunt Patty got through to them. No-one can say no to her." He put one arm around her.

She laughed. "True, but what happened, really?"

"They came in this morning and sat me down. They had explained about what happened to your nan and reckon that I can't be in two places at once. They also got some results from the forensics. The time of death looks like it was really early on Saturday morning." He whispered the last bit, and Esther jerked back.

"What?"

"Yeah, so they reluctantly admitted that it probably wasn't me. I have an alibi for Saturday morning anyway. I was with Will."

"Oh, I'm so happy that you're out. Was it horrible?"

"It wasn't too bad. My dad used to take me hunting when I was young, so I'm used to sleeping in random places. At least it was dry where they held me. The worst part was the boredom. I was always humming or singing softly. Luckily, they can't take away my voice."

"Yeah."

He slumped down at one of the tables and crossed his leg over. Ashton took a beer bottle from the middle of the table, and lifted it up to clink with hers.

"I'm exhausted, mate, but I couldn't miss the gig! Even if I had to break out of prison." He grinned.

"I am so glad you're here. Are you alright with these songs?"

"I'll sing whatever you like."

Esther's eyes flicked over the tables. You could usually tell the music lovers because they looked over often, attention caught by the song. Their feet moved along in time, almost as if of their own accord.

Tonight, she was afraid people had already had too much to drink. An old man she thought was Troy's uncle was shuffling around in a liberal expression of the word dance. Troy's friends' table were calling for more wine, although by the number of bottles on the table, they had had enough.

Esther tapped her feet to get the beat. She started to play the opening bars of Walk the Line, feeling the music flow through her and those warm feelings of singing with her nan. Ashton turned towards her, a grin spreading over his face. He leaned in and sung the chorus with her.

She thought about what to play next, but felt her fingers playing the start of I won't back down, by Tom Petty and the Heartbreakers. She took it up an octave and Ashton looked over at her questioningly, but joined in with his rich tenor.

As she played, she thought about how she hoped the truth would come out. She wished so desperately that the killer would be found.

Concentrate, she told herself. She plucked the strings and came up to the climax of the song. The ukelele seemed to take on a life of its own, almost as if it was challenging her to play faster.

People turned their heads toward her, and Aria's dad paused, with his beer almost at his mouth. A line of ale dripped into his lap.

At this point, she was almost wrestling with the ukelele, which was humming with energy. She tried to hold the final note, but couldn't keep it up. She was afraid the ukelele would fly out of her hands. She cut it off all of a sudden, and bent over, breathing heavily.

Ashton raised his eyebrows at her.

"Just cover for me," she mouthed at him, giving him a

flap of the hand. Then she gripped the ukelele tight and managed to wrestle it into its case, snapping the lid shut with a click.

She looked over, and Ashton was bowing elaborately. "Thanks everyone, we have been Soulful tonight. We hope we brought a little soul to the engaged couple. We are available to book for weddings, too. Just saying."

In the silence, someone clapped. Once. Aria stood up and cheered.

As Esther straightened, still clutching her case, Jayden walked up to her. "You're really talented," he said. "I didn't think you had it in you. A few interesting dance moves, though. I got it on vid."

Esther was left with her mouth open, as Jayden walked away. "Thanks, I think," she murmured.

"Just ignore him, mate," Ashton said. "Now what *was* that?"

"I'll tell you later," she said, packing up her music folder. She bent down to pack the stand down, then looked up as the best man stood, drink in hand.

"What now?" Ashton mouthed.

"No idea," she said.

"I just want to say," he said. Someone tugged at his jacket to get him to sit down. "If you don't know me, I'm Bradley."

"We've already had the speeches," Aria's dad murmured, in a low voice.

"I'm just going to say that I've always loved Aria, and I bloody hope that Troy looks after her. I've finally given up all hope of ever being that person." He paused. "In fact, we spent one night together—"

Somebody swiped the microphone off him, and Troy's mother said," Sit down."

"Drunk!" Aria's dad said.

Esther thought it couldn't be true, as her friend had never mentioned it. She looked over at the head table. Aria went sort of pale, slumped down in her chair, and shrugged off her dad's hand. Then changed her mind, lifted her skirts off the ground and stalked out of the room. Esther left her stuff there and ran after her.

"It's no big deal. I never thought Troy was good enough for her." Aria's dad mumbled it, but Esther heard loud and clear.

"At least I wouldn't do anything to make money," Troy said. "Eh, Jayden?" Esther turned back. She was almost at the door. The mood in the room felt dangerous.

Jayden stood up and took a step towards his friend. "Why do you think that? Anything I do is for love. It doesn't seem to make much difference what I do, though."

His wife flicked her blonde hair behind her shoulder furiously, stood up and left the room.

Esther met Clark's eyes across the room in perfect understanding. He walked towards her.

Not now, she thought. *I've got to go and see my friend.*

Clark stopped in the middle of the room, winked at her and called out, "Something to dance to!" Someone switched on the Monster Mash, and he started dancing, until he was joined by three or four of the little siblings and cousins. As she watched, one of them clamped onto his leg.

"Thank you," she mouthed. But what she was thinking was 'I bloody love you'.

Aria was sitting on the bench outside the hall. Esther plopped down next to her. Her friend's mascara was smudged but she had a grim look on her face.

She sighed. "It's not illegal, is it?"

"So you and him?" Esther asked.

"It was ages ago."

"Of course it's not illegal. I think it's the fact that you didn't tell anybody about it."

"Why the heck is he telling people about it now?" she asked.

That was a good question. Something had happened back there, and while she didn't have time to examine it right now, a tiny tingle at the back of her neck reminded her of that night at the quilting club. Unexplained things. Mysterious things.

Her ukelele had buzzed with life, had gone rogue, almost as if it was possessed. Then people blurted out their secrets?

"It sounds like he is in love with you," she said. When Aria didn't answer, she asked, "You knew?"

"He told me, but of course I told him there is no chance." Aria fiddled with her skirt.

"All you can do is talk to Troy about it. He is a pretty relaxed sort of guy. He might be completely fine."

Aria was quiet for a moment. "I like the look of your policeman. When are you going to ask him out? Is that why you're so keen to get the case over and done with?"

"Stop," she said.

"He watches you all the time. And when you were performing, he had this sloppy smile on his face."

Esther smiled a secret smile. It was better to be honest late than never. Sometimes, it was about being honest with yourself. She was a witch.

She shivered, thinking of the instrument buzzing with life. This time, she was sure she had made it happen.

"You're cold, Essie. Let's go back in."

Esther went to get a drink for Clark. She was enjoying the music as she grabbed one of the beers from the bar. Her skin rippled into goosebumps, and she often thought that type of visceral reaction was like a bewitching of her body, a song that reached into her soul and possessed her mood.

"You dance?" she said, holding the drink out.

"Oh, well, only if I have to." He stepped one foot in front of the other and slid the other one behind, turning around. A grin spread over his face as he moved his shoulders to the rhythm. He could dance, alright.

She laughed. "Lies. You love it."

"A little. And you seem to love solving cases."

"That reminds me, do any of our suspects have a passion for cycling?"

"I'll have a look later."

He reached for her hands and pulled her in a little closer, so that she was forced to match his movements. With light fingers, he brushed her hair back from her face and tucked it behind her ear.

"You're pretty amazing, you know," he said. His fingers curled around behind her shoulder, and his rough thumb stroked the top of her arm. "I saw the way you've listened to everyone. Lord knows it's easy to get bitter when you're dealing with these sorts of investigations. To switch off. To just want the whole thing over and done with."

She looked over his shoulder and was happy to see Aria talking with Troy on the dance floor. At least her friend wasn't watching.

She thought of how tough these last few weeks had been. What had kept her motivated all this time?

A gentle finger tilted her chin up and he brought his

face close to hers, nose to nose. Up this close she could see the way one eyebrow thinned in the middle, like there had been a scar beneath at some stage. She noticed a sprinkling of freckles across his face and stubble on his cheeks. His hair was all shades from blonde to reddish brown to deep russet and even one or two greys.

His eyes drunk in her eyes, hair, face, falling to her lips. She felt her heart start to race as his face nudged hers and she moved her mouth to his. Their lips fit together. It was a soft kiss, a testing.

He pulled back, hazel eyes burning into her. "Was that okay?"

She liked seeing him unsure, when he was normally in charge. "Hmm," she said, biting her lip. Then a smile burst through. "Yes."

He leaned forwards and suddenly seemed very big. Esther melted into him, her pulse racing overtime, and he kissed her thoroughly, right there on the dance floor.

A while later, after helping Aria and her family to clean up, she arrived home at her flat. The kitten had only knocked one flowerpot off the windowsill and tiny dirty footprints tracked across the kitchen floor. The bird was, thankfully, still alive.

She took the ukelele and thrust it firmly under her drawers. The diabolical instrument and the case would have to wait until after her trip to Paunceworthy.

CHAPTER 22

"$\mathcal{M}$r Bauer, are you sure you're going to be alright looking after the cat and the bird for a few days?"

Esther had packed her bag that morning after a quick breakfast of toast and jam, served with a strong coffee. The kitten watched her from on top of a folded jersey.

Mr Bauer brushed off her questions. "Yes, yes, it's fine. Don't you worry. I never thought I'd say this but I actually think the cat has calmed down a bit since living with you."

"The bird eats leftover veges and some seeds. Louis' tins are in the cupboard above the fridge. Sometimes, he decides he won't eat it, so then I give him salmon."

"Yeah, that's good. That's fine." He waved her away.

With one last glance at the flat, she opened the car

189

door, and put her bag in. A beating of wings came from behind her, and the bird flew into the car and settled on the back of the passenger seat, its head tilted to the side.

"Out," she said, but it was half-hearted, as the bird had never once listened to her so far.

Mr Bauer laughed. "I think it wants to go on a road trip."

"I never thought my life would be ruled by half a pet shop," she grumbled. "It's just you and the cat then. See you soon. Ring me if there are any issues."

She went to pick up her nan, crunching up the frosty path to the rest home.

"Are you ready?"

"I'm more than ready. Can you help me with the bags, dear?"

Esther picked up the purple bags and carried them out through the wide hallways. She signed her nan out.

"You have a lovely Christmas, Hope," said the receptionist. "Look after her."

"I will."

Esther opened up the boot and lifted the bags in.

Her nan opened up the passenger door. The bird flew straight for her nan's face, then alighted softly onto her shoulder. The old woman turned her face towards the bird and when she turned back there was a tear in her eye.

"My old familiar."

If Esther had any capacity left for surprise, she would have been shocked right now. As it was, she simply asked a question. "Your old what?"

"My demon. It left me when I no longer used my magic. It must be back now for you!" Her nan clapped her hands together and it hopped slightly.

Esther frowned. "Are you sure it's not just a normal bird?"

"I'm sure. How long has it been around and has it helped you at all?"

"Probably only a week." Esther thought back to the many times she had seen the bird. She'd found the Bluejay poster after he came inside the first time. Had he tried to show her things other times?

"He said he tried but, every single time, he was attacked by that kitten of yours."

"What?"

"He said he stole the poster from the bookshop and brought it to you." Esther stood there with her mouth open.

She couldn't even form the question, 'how do you know', as she didn't think she wanted the answer. If this bird had stolen the poster from Book Ends, how did it get there in the first place?

She asked her nan about the poster. "When was the last time you saw it?"

"That poster must have got caught up in one of my

books. I totally forgot that your parents sold my books there when I moved into the home. Come on, love, let's get in the car."

The drive to Paunceworthy was spent in good spirits. Esther and her Nan sang along to songs and talked about unexplained things.

"So, this Vicky is the psychic?"

"It seems like it."

"And she was actually talking to her husband?"

"Well, I don't know. I honestly don't. But how else did she know that we had some evidence against her?"

Her nan shook her head. "Suspicious."

"That Kevin man said he would miss me while I'm gone," her nan said.

"The bossy one?"

"That very same," she said, with a smile. "Oh, he's not too bad, I suppose. He does try to get me involved in the activities."

"He sounds like a good friend to you, Nan."

As they drove down the lane lined with walnut trees, Esther got that familiar sick feeling in the pit of her stomach. Was she ready for all the questions? No, she didn't have a 'proper career'. No, she wasn't successful. She hadn't even solved the blooming mystery. And she didn't have a boyfriend.

But she did have a Clark. She wasn't sure what they

were to each other right yet, but it felt like something was starting.

"Try not to think about the crime too much while we're away, love."

"I'll try not to," she said.

They arrived late on Christmas Eve, to find Paunceworthy going mad. Cars thronged the main street, and people crossed the road without looking.

Esther pulled over and rolled her window down. "Excuse me," she asked an elderly woman, who was rushing across the road, with a disgruntled looking man following along behind her. "What's going on?"

"Oh, we're having a little bit of excitement here. The new mayor decided not to put up the Christmas decorations. We've been writing him letters, which he ignored, and now we are making a wee commotion."

"On Christmas Eve?"

"Why ever not?" She walked a couple of steps closer. "Aren't you Paula's daughter?"

She heaved a sigh and her grandmother patted her knee. It had started and she'd just arrived in town. "Yup."

"She drafted up the letter for us. It helps having a judge on our side."

"Good luck with your protest," she said, and wound up the window. "Come on, Paula's mum. Let's get to the house."

When they got to the house, her aunties and cousins were already in the lounge and her Uncle John was coming out of the kitchen, two beers sloshing around in the bottles as he squeezed past.

"You alright, Esther?" he asked.

"Hi," she said, weak in the face of an overwhelm of relatives and Christmas cheer.

"Mum, I wasn't expecting all these people to be here yet," she said, from the corner of her mouth. It might be a bit much for Nan."

"Nonsense," her mum said, Her brown bob streaked with grey seemed even more severe than it had last time she saw her. "Your nan is fine."

One of her brother's kids offered her a mince pie.

"Thanks," she said, brightly. Was that Sophie or Soraya?

"I didn't like it," the girl said, and Esther noticed an edge that looked particularly slobbered on. She put the pie down on the bench.

"For later," she assured her.

Her mum was arranging crackers and cheese on a platter. "Hello, darling. Doesn't look like it's too much for her." She gestured to where Nan was in a circle of people, telling them a story with expansive movements, the jewels on her fingers flashing in the light. A few decorations were hung around the walls, and a small tree sat on the dresser.

Esther ducked into the relative quiet of the kitchen, stepping around her mother as she reached for the knife block. Suddenly she realized she'd had enough of dancing around subjects in this house.

"So, Mum, what's the big secret?"

"What big secret?" she said. It was the same tone of voice she'd use if Esther tried to ask about what case she was working on. Every part of her life had its compartment, and may the gods defend whoever mixed them up. Work, home life, charity work, tennis.

"Oh, you know, nan told me that you made her promise not to tell me who I am!"

Everything went quiet. Esther looked suspiciously out the door. The aunties were playing a game of cards, while her nan watched, and her younger cousins were looking at the TV, which was showing a home renovation program.

"We will talk about this later," Esther whispered.

"Alright," her mum said, spreading her hands. "You've had dinner?"

"Yep, I had a burger on the way," she answered, knowing it wouldn't be the last time she was asked that.

"I'm going to take Nan along to the spare bedroom."

"Hello sweetheart," her dad said, leaning in for a scratchy kiss on the cheek. "Do you need some dinner?"

"No thanks, dad," she said. "I've got a bird now, apparently, too."

"Here, I'll take those." He took the bags off her and started walking up the stairs. "The bird can stay in the conservatory."

Esther carried the bird through the house to the conservatory. She opened the window at the top, so that it could fly in and out.

"Here you go."

It flew off and landed on the back of the cane chair.

She went back out to the lounge, found a spot in the corner and listened to her Uncle John's stories. Hope told them about Esther and Ashton playing at the rest home, and her mum looked over at her, thoughtfully.

Eventually everyone else moved off and somehow, Esther was left looking at her phone, when her Mum stood up to take the tray out.

"You're distracted tonight."

"Yeah." Her mother always seemed to state things as fact, when Esther felt she should be asking. Emotions and thoughts were twisty and nebulous, not bright red building blocks. *Why don't you ask how I'm feeling?* She thought.

She followed her mum out to the kitchen and helped

her with the dishes, and 1970's music blasted from the radio.

When the job was done, her mum wiped the sink down carefully, then hung the tea towels over the rack, lining them up. She turned to Esther.

"Come with me." Esther's heart started to race. Would her mum tell her everything? Her mother went up the stairs and stopped in the hallway. She faced away from the bedrooms and hummed a note. Then two more. It sounded unfinished to Esther, like an A minor broken chord. She put her hands on her hips.

"Is it really time for Christmas carols?"

"Shh," her mother said. She looked as if she was listening. Esther followed her gaze and saw two huge cupboard doors made of some dark wood. She was sure they had never been there before.

"Were they always…" she murmured.

"Of course," her mother said. "You just have to know the right pitch."

She opened up one of the doors and stood aside.

"Go on, then."

Pushing away the feelings that this was the start of a horror movie scene, Esther took a breath and ducked her head to step into the darkness.

It smelled a little musty. Her mum came in after her and shut the door behind. What next? Was she going to magic up a candle from thin air?

Esther was almost disappointed when her mum switched on the light and wooden walls appeared around her.

"We think it was a servant's corridor or some sort of larder," her mum said. In front of them was a door.

Another pop of the lights and a room full of diamonds appeared in front of her. *No, not diamonds,* she thought to herself. Sparkly costumes with feathers, sequins and jewels.

Esther felt herself drawn towards the beautiful fabrics, and picked up one of the dresses, which felt scaly and cool.

The room wasn't much bigger than her parent's ensuite. The hanger took up one wall and the other wall was full of boxes and a wooden chest, with hats, scarves, gloves and bags piled on top.

"See, I was proud of her," said her mum.

"This all belonged to Nan?" she asked.

"Yes. Some of the things in the boxes are our old mementos from when you were young, though."

"Were you ever going to show me?"

"Of course." Her mother's tone was stung. She let out a breath. "It just never felt like the right time."

Esther sat down on one of the boxes, picking up the hat that was on top and putting it on her head. It smelled like mothballs.

"There's no such thing as the perfect time, Mum."

Her mum looked at her. "How come you didn't tell me you played at the rest home?"

Esther sighed. "It's… not the sort of thing that interests you."

Her mum moved the accessories off the top of the chest, and Esther felt her eyes start to burn with allergies, as dust rose up.

"Oh, I'm going to sneeze. Can't you do something about the dust?"

"I don't have a magic wand. It's not like that." She opened the chest and pulled out a stack of photographs. "Should be somewhere in here."

"This is what I was after," she said. "It was a Christmas function at the kindergarten, actually, and you would have been four years old."

She passed across an old photo, which showed Esther in a huge crown, and her nan in the same.

"Oh, that is classic," Esther said, and pulled out her phone to take a snap of it.

"You were an interesting child," her mum said, drily.

"I made Nan wear that, didn't I? I wanted to be the three kings, because that was my favourite carol."

"Mm. One of the dads," she said, pointing to a man on the left, who was sort of leaning in, "dressed up in a Santa suit, but he smelt of beer, since he'd been at his work lunch. You kids didn't notice, though. They did the presents and a lolly scramble."

Her mother's mouth tightened. "Well, it would have been about fifteen minutes after that photo was taken. I had to leave to pick up Phil from school."

"You and your nan were singing carols along with everyone else. But you got bored and wandered onto the playground and jumped off, but for some reason, you landed on your head. Mum saw what was happening, and panicked, and she knew she could heal you with music, so she kept singing, as loud as she could."

"The head teacher saw it all, though, the fall, the blood, you jumping up like nothing was wrong. And through it all, your grandmother, carrying on singing like some sort of psychopath. It was absolute chaos."

"Oh."

"The teacher thought I should ban Mum from ever seeing you again." She sighed and waved her hand around. "Now, the next bit I'm not proud of, but I was so wild. I made her promise never to use magic around you again, or speak of it. You have to understand that her singing and all that went along with it, had always made everything… difficult."

If she wasn't so upset, she might have thought it was a little ironic that her mother had made such a huge emotional decision about her daughter's life, when her own power was taking the emotion out of a decision.

"What should she have done differently?"

"What do you mean? It was all so long ago."

"I mean, if you were there, would you have stopped her from healing me, since there were people watching?"

Her mother looked surprised. "I suppose not."

"How come you never told me? Could you have removed the vow?" Paula sighed, and Esther wondered again how much she had given up for the family. For her. But also for her job. Her profile.

"I did what I did to protect you. You don't want a childhood like mine. We can't go back."

She recognized something of her mother in herself, maybe for the first time. She had often felt the weight of expectations. She knew she had spent years running away from that feeling of not quite measuring up.

It was true that they couldn't go back. But she had to make peace with it somehow.

How were you supposed to know what was right, if you had nothing to model from? Not nothing, she told herself. She could choose the best parts of what her mother had given her. She supposed that was stability, dependability.

She could also take the best parts of what others had given her; her father had shown her what hard-working selflessness was. Her brothers had taught her things too, and loved her in their own way. And, of course, Hope had shown her kindness and beautiful, unconditional love.

CHAPTER 23

Esther woke up in the bed of her childhood, a single bed formed to her body. The curtains let in a lot of light, which made her squint, and a dog was barking. The bed head was painted white with a few stickers stuck to it. She looked up, expecting to see the pictures of boy bands on the wall, but they were long gone.

She couldn't help but think of the people who wouldn't be seeing their loved ones this Christmas. Harry Deed. Phoebe. Greg.

She could see that Rochelle was just trying to do her best with the bookshop too. It had been her dad's dream, and she had spent her life trying to live up to that. But it had ultimately made her bitter.

She wondered what would happen to the bookshop.

She didn't have any control over that, but hoped it would stay open.

"Morning, dear," her dad said. He was cooking bacon and eggs in the frying pan and the delicious smells hit her nose as she came in. "Breakfast is almost ready."

"Looks done to me," she said, eyeing the black around the edges.

"Alright, alright."

Her brother emerged from his room, no doubt drawn by the smell of bacon.

"Hey Phil," she said, studying him to see if she could sense anything witchy. His hair was even longer and more unwashed than last time, and she thought he was even wearing the same hoodie. "How's life?"

Phil mumbled something back.

"He's working for a very progressive company where they can work from home a lot of the time," her mum put in. "It's really great."

When they were finished, she went into the kitchen to load the dishwasher. Her mum bustled through with an armload of sheets towards the laundry.

"So when are we going to get into the… you know what?"

"What?"

"Well, if we are witches, when do we get to the hocus pocus, cauldrons and burning sage? I'm looking forward to magicking my hay fever away for one thing."

"I hate to disappoint you," her mother said, the edges of her mouth twitching. "The most magical thing today is going to be keeping the whole extended family from killing each other."

"Don't even say that," she said, with a shudder.

"Oh, sorry, dear. Bit close to home." Her mother checked on the round pudding below its wrap. "Now, I could use some help with whipping the cream. But first, let's have a little tipple."

As Esther sipped her bubbles, she thought again of the memories and why they had only come back to her now. Some of them were really significant events in her life. Memories were stronger when they were attached to emotions, weren't they? And her mother's magic worked by removing emotions.

She saw what she now realised was a ghost outside their window, being set free. Someone from the Titanic. Was her magic communicating with spirits?

"You look a million miles away, Esther."

"Did you do something to make me forget? Like you did to your friend Matty all those years ago?" She blurted it out.

Her mother stared at her, one hand on her hip. "Matty's husband was an abusive fool. It was the only way she could leave him."

"So you helped her leave?"

"Yes." She put down her glass and bundled the sheets

into a ball. "I didn't make you forget. Just associate less emotion with the memories. A mother is allowed to sing to their child, aren't they?"

"I'm strong enough to deal with it, now."

Her mother didn't seem to hear her. She thrust the sheets into the machine and came back through.

"Now, don't say anything yet. I've been in touch with the principal of the local high school. We've been in Rotary together for a few years, and he needs someone to help out in the music department. I talked you up to him, and he is very impressed. It would be a very good stepping stone, even if only for a couple of years. And it would save you doing shifts here and there, all over the place. You could come and live here, not necessarily at home — although you are welcome — but in town?"

Esther searched her mother's face. She seemed a little embarrassed about showing she missed her daughter.

"Mum, that's so kind," she said. Her mother smiled and held her champagne flute up.

As Esther clinked her glass with her mother's, she felt a warm glow around her breastbone, thinking that her mum had said nice things about her, and managed to get her a job opportunity that might be good for her career. She was tempted. Life would be so easy.

"We can figure out this magic thing together." Her mum looked down, the tapping of her little finger the only sign of any inner turmoil.

She thought of Ashton, the practises spent jamming, getting lost in the music, laughing, joking. The way he remembered things for her. The way he was always there for her.

She thought of Ledstow. A town that was held together by the love and magic of its citizens. A town that was a haven for those that struggled to fit in elsewhere.

A certain tall man with kind, intelligent hazel eyes and a tattoo that had a story waiting to be told.

In Paunceworthy, she was always Paula's daughter. Was she a bad kid for wanting to live in another town? Perhaps she needed to learn who she was when she wasn't trying to be someone else's version of success.

Who was the person she wanted to be without anyone else's expectations? What was her own version of success? She had to figure it out on her own, with the help of her nan, a kitten and an extremely weird bird.

"I think I'm needed in Ledstow for a little while longer," she said.

CHAPTER 24

$\mathcal{E}$sther arrived back in Ledstow on a bright but cool morning. The lake shone on her left and the village came into view as she came around the bottom of the hills. There was the old manor halfway up the hillside, the tiny stone church, and the houses in a huddle below.

"Thank you, again, for convincing your mother to get rid of that dratted vow," her nan said. "I'll be able to show you a few things."

"I'm hoping it means she trusts us?" Esther was thrilled when she thought about learning magic with her grandmother.

After dropping her nan off, she went back to her apartment. The bird flew in when she opened the door.

Esther unpacked her things. She sat down on her bed,

and as she did, her eyes fell on the chest of drawers and the bright case underneath. She pulled out her ukulele.

Turning it over in her hands, she looked carefully at it. Something had definitely been wrong with it at the party, and she looked inside, just in case someone was playing a trick on her. With what, though?

She held it up to her ear, and plucked a string, experimentally. In the sound, she thought she heard the word, 'please'. Her legs went cold. Maybe she should wait until someone else was here with her. But she had seen Vicky speaking to her very dead husband. She had seen it with her own eyes.

"Rochelle?" she whispered, feeling like a fool. Every hair on her body was standing on end.

As she listened, words came into her head that seemed so familiar, as if they had been played over and over in her sleep. She grabbed a pen and her notebook and wrote the words, 'I'm listening now.'

In the silence, the bird scratched around in the tray of seeds she had left for it.

Her hand started moving across the page.

I was never very good with technology. I can't write words on a screen from here.

I tried talking to Greg. He convinced himself that he was crazy. Esther remembered the way Greg had stared into the distance while saying Rochelle was in every decoration on the Christmas tree. The way he had shaken his head, as if to rid himself of unwelcome thoughts. The way he just wanted to get back to work.

I tried talking to Phoebe, but she thought it was her great grandfather. Esther thought back to what Phoebe had said, that she was so frightened of her relative. She wouldn't have wanted to listen.

Jo was too busy to notice. Esther smiled. Jo had said they were losing things all the time. Was Rochelle trying to move objects to communicate?

I know you can hear me, Esther. Follow the music.

She waited, but that was all that came to her. *Gee, thanks for the help,* she thought. Follow the music? That is what I do, anyway.

The bird flew over to her, alighting on her arm. It leaned its head down towards her, almost like it was saying, 'well done'.

"You knew what was happening all along, didn't you, Jay?" She lightly stroked along its back. "Are you really a familiar? Good birdie."

It flew off. Esther flopped back on the bed, and stared at the ceiling for a while. She picked up her phone. Clark answered, voice muffled like his mouth was full.

"Hello? Sorry, I'm eating pudding."

"At eleven in the morning?"

"There's nothing wrong with that. Didn't want to miss your call," he said.

Esther smiled. "Did you have a good Christmas?"

"The usual, actually. I ate way too much and my dad started telling offensive jokes. Triss loved it though."

"Oh well, that's what these few days are for. Unwinding from the hangover and pecking at the left-over dessert." *Getting over the fact that half of my very business-focused and hardworking family is magical. Including me,* she thought with a thrill.

"I'm actually working right now."

"Are you?"

"I've got a lot of paperwork to do. Two weeks' worth, probably."

"I hope you've got time to discuss the case. I think we've got a lead on who may be a suspect from the party. We've just got to figure out why."

"Yeah, definitely. Lots to discuss. I'll meet you at the local tonight?"

"How come you're so busy with paperwork all of a sudden?"

"No reason."

She thought he sounded like he was hiding something. "Come on, tell me."

"Alright, well… I had to bargain with Shona to release your mate before the engagement party. She didn't believe that he was innocent."

"Really?" Despite a little twinge that the Detective had been so set on Ashton being guilty, Esther was undeniably happy.

Aria arrived that afternoon and enveloped her in a hug. She passed a gift across, then walked in, looking around her.

"Where's my little baby boo boo?"

"He's on the bed," Esther said, and folded her leg under her on the couch.

Aria walked back in with Louis tucked into the crook of her elbow, a purring ball of happiness.

"Open it, hurry up."

Esther eyed her, wondering why she was so excited, but picked up the red and white bundle. "How did the talk with Troy go?"

"The talk went fine," Aria said, sitting down. "The days after weren't so great. Dad and Troy hardly talked during Christmas dinner. Troy's mum organised some 'party games' — you know that one where you have to tie a balloon around your waist and the other person has to pop it without using their hands?" She whistled. "It did not end well."

"Oh no," Esther said.

"Troy fell into the pile of presents and broke the very expensive plate his parents had bought for us."

"Oops," she laughed, sliding her fingers under the edge of the wrapping paper.

"Just tear it off!"

Esther lifted the soft material out of the wrapper. The fabric inside was a blue silk threaded with gold and green flowers. Embroidered birds caught mid-flight floated in the spaces between.

"Oh, I love it!"

"It's got the vibes of a great British detective. Plus you're obviously into birds now."

Esther put the robe on, wrapping the silky fabric around her. She wouldn't quite say she was 'into birds'. But she appreciated the thought Aria had put into the present. Gift giving was almost like her friend's magic power.

"Thank you. I got you something, too. It's not wrapped, because of the—"

"Environment," Aria finished.

"Yeah." Esther picked up the glasses case, which she had personalised with the words, 'I see more clearly in my dreams', and passed it across. "For those designer sunnies."

"Aww perfect. I do, though!"

"I know you do."

Esther smiled when she saw Clark's tall form stoop under the doorway of the pub a little later. There was a pleasant buzz of people in the Twig and Berries, and she and Ashton were watching the band set up.

"I'll get this round," Ash said, and weaved his way through the tables.

Clark stood next to her, his arm lightly touching hers. "She didn't do it. Vicky."

Esther sighed. "I think I knew that. I just don't know where to go next. It's got to be someone either big enough to overpower Rochelle or smart and sneaky enough."

"Mm. It's not a straightforward thing, at all. That's for sure."

"What do you mean?"

"Well, you know how I'm investigating paranormal phenomena? That was why I was interested in this case." He kept his voice low.

"Why? What was paranormal about it?" Her heart skipped a beat or two as she wondered what he would say about her own contact with the other side.

"A message in the bookshop. Written in the deceased's handwriting."

"Rochelle's?"

He nodded. "Shona made me rub it off right away. Apparently, it was written after she died. Unless our forensic scientist is wrong, and he's never wrong."

Written after she died? Two weeks ago, Esther would have laughed in his face. Now, though, it was par for the course. Of course Rochelle had written a message. She could never use technology. "What did it say?"

"'Join two halves.' That's all."

"Why didn't you tell me earlier?"

"I didn't think it really made much difference to the case." She narrowed her eyes at him, but he seemed genuine.

"You really are bad at this stuff. Two halves of what?"

He shrugged. "Alright, I'll give you the rundown on what happened with Vicky. She was taken in for questioning, but released pretty quickly."

"I asked if she met with Rochelle that evening. She did, but she only lied because she didn't want to look guilty."

"Whereabouts?"

"At the shop. She said Rochelle really wanted one of the books she took in. I'm not sure why. In the end, she refused to sell that one to her, although she took a few of the others."

"It was this book. But the suspect — I mean, Victoria — reckoned that there was a small scrap of paper inside that was more important." He searched on his phone and showed her the book. It was an old book about gardening. "We don't have the piece of paper. She doesn't know where it is."

"A scrap of paper? All this over a message on a scrap of paper?"

"Not even a message." He took a long sip of his drink. "It was music, apparently. Well, it was half of a piece of music."

Clark saw her face. "What?" He asked.

But a cold feeling had overcome her. She shook her head.

"Is this about your talents?"

She looked up sharply.

"I saw you at the engagement party, remember. You are an amazing musician and you seemed to really put a spell on the audience."

"She puts on a good show, doesn't she?" Ashton put in, setting the glasses down on the table.

Esther breathed out. "Yes, that's it. I think this whole investigation is blocking my creativity, when it comes to singing."

She put her fingers on her temples, trying to think. A song on a scrap of paper. Her nan!

She looked at Clark, remembering how he had been willing to open up to her and took a deep breath, holding for a second and then letting go. "Actually, no. That's not quite all."

CHAPTER 25

Esther's heart was hammering in her chest but she went into the bookshop.

"I just came in to see if you need any help."

"Thank you," Jo said, with real feeling. They were slugging back instant coffee as if it was pure energy. "The few days after Christmas are just as bad as before. Only with fewer carols. Get stuck in at the till, if you like."

She waved at the line of people who were waiting to be served, and Jayden who was scanning books.

"Blue cover. Romance with enemies to lovers? I think you mean this one," Jo said.

When it was break time, she went into the back room, and made herself a tea. Jayden was in there, scrolling through his phone so fast she was surprised he didn't get thumb cramps.

She sat down. "Hey," she said, and every hair stood up on her body, knowing that she was likely next to a killer. "Would you mind, um, showing me how to make a Story?"

He reached over. "Just tap here, then get the photo or video you want."

"It's the second one. Just there." Esther watched as Jayden glanced at the poster of the Bluejay with the missing piece and his eyes widened. She'd gone home and checked the poster just to be certain. Sure enough, there were a few notes in faded writing in the corner.

"It's my grandmother's and apparently, she will pay a lot of money to get the little ripped off piece back. Must be a collector's edition poster or something. She got me to put it in a safe," she said.

All credit to him, Esther thought, he didn't do much more than blink, although he must have been itching to steal the phone off her.

"It's your grandmother's," he said.

"Yeah, so I'll post it on here and hopefully the person will get in touch with me, all anonymous of course."

He nodded.

Esther left the shop at three. "I hope I've helped a bit. I'm going to walk home through the park."

Heart racing, she went down the front steps and turned right. She crossed the road, noticing Clark slumped down in a car outside the park gates.

Would he take the bait? She found a park bench and put her bag down. Too late, she saw that she'd put the wrong book in her bag this morning. She had found The Making of a Performer under the couch and thought she could drop it back to Cara at the library afterwards. But her hand touched Murder Investigation for Dumbos, which was way too obvious with its bright cover. *Oh no*, she thought, with a sinking heart, she had spoiled everything. The butterflies flitting in her stomach became squirming worms.

She looked into the bushes, hoping Clark was there somewhere.

"We'll be right there," he had said. "Trust me. And Shona and Derek too." Derek was another policeman, a short man with large ears, who looked almost ready for retirement.

It didn't take very long until something happened. Esther felt a tugging on her shoulder and her bag came loose. She screamed in reflex.

"Open it!" Jayden said, leaning in towards her. He was wearing a stocking over his head, but he hadn't bothered to change his top.

"What?"

"Open your phone! Now!"

With shaking fingers, she put in the security pin and slowly handed the phone back.

Jayden tore off across the clearing. Clark burst from

the greenery in chase, and jumped for his ankles. Both men went down in a pile of bags and clothes.

Clark twisted his arm behind his back and stood him up. Shona arrived on the scene and cuffed him.

By the time Esther got over there, he had stopped struggling. The stocking was off his head, and Jayden stood, slumped, between them. Clark was sweating slightly and Shona had her hands on her hips.

"We've been looking into you, Jayden Shortridge," Clark said. "We know you didn't want to be a YouTuber. You just wanted to take your photos of landscapes and wildlife. But your wife wanted you to be an influencer, and bring in the big bucks. You'd do anything to live up to her vision of you, wouldn't you? She told us that once you stole an old guy's wallet and filmed him to see how long it took 'til he noticed. We know you weren't at home all night on that Friday. That puts you squarely in the crosshairs. You better tell us what happened with Rochelle."

"My wife ratted me out?"

"Talk!"

"Alright, you obviously know it was me. My YouTube channel is doing well and Rochelle seems to get in a lot of fights. People love that stuff. On that Friday, I hid in the shop, so I could record. But bloody Phoebe came in early."

"Then Rochelle met Vicky outside, that evening,

instead of the next day. She brought the books in and Rochelle was really interested in this one particular book. Vicky decided not to sell it. It got a bit heated. A bird flew in to the shop, and caused all sorts of trouble, so I couldn't hear what was going on."

It sounded like Rochelle had seen the full poster, then Jay had flown in and ripped it while delivering it to her.

"I thought it must have been a first edition book or something. It was just some boring gardening book, but I was invested by then. And stuck."

"After Vicky left, Rochelle was researching this old-fashioned singer. It turns out the old bird lives here in town."

A chill went up Esther's spine.

"There was some old blog about a person that had been healed by watching one of her performances. I'm always looking for something I can sell, and I thought if I could get that, it would be worth it. Sounds like Rochelle only wanted it to heal her dog's tumour."

"Rochelle went back over to Vicky's really late that night, must have been about midnight, and I followed her. I recorded the conversation. She demanded the book, and said she wanted to know where the poster was. Vicky gave in. You know how weak she is." He scowled.

"I waited until she was almost back at the shop. Then I took the slip of paper and left the book. Vicky wanted it to look younger. At least I was going to sell it to other people, not just use it myself."

"Rochelle was so angry when I confronted her. She didn't take well to being told I'd filmed her."

"So you killed her?"

"I made her tell me about it, first. Then she managed to knock me onto the ground. I knew it was going to be one of us."

"Righto, mate, you're out of here."

Derek put Jayden in his police car out on the main road. People walking down the road turned and stared. Esther knew it would be all over town by the end of the day. Helped, no doubt, by the quilt club.

"Foolish boy," her nan had said, when Esther spoke to her last night. "So that young man was the one that came in here after me?"

"Yes."

"Do you know the most ridiculous thing?"

"What?"

"He likely wouldn't be able to use the song at all," she said. "I could. And likely Paula could, and perhaps yourself. You need to be magical to wield a song like that."

Esther sighed. Clark came over to her, brushing the leaves off his clothes.

"We make a pretty good pair," he said.

"Mm, a professor and a retail assistant," she whispered.

"It is intriguing, though, that your grandmother wrote a song that was thought to heal people. It's the sort of thing my research focuses on."

"She's a very special lady. I wouldn't put anything past her."

"Would you like to tell me more over lunch one day?"

"I would," she said. Life wasn't a musical, Esther reflected. Sometimes families had secrets. Sometimes people who cared about each other changed and twisted the truth. People lied about who they were. But friends stood by each other. And love sparked in the messiest of circumstances. "But not today. I'm going home to see my kitten. And you've got paperwork to do."

THE END

A NOTE FROM K M JACKWAYS

Hello! I hope you enjoyed Murder for a Song. For this book, I wanted to write a story about families of all sorts. You can find these characters in the next book, Death and a Duet.

Many thanks to my wonderful beta readers, Diane Lewis and Catherine Langford, for reading the bare bones and the wonderful comments that had me laughing in the middle of the night. Thanks always to my lovely husband for encouraging me through the dark times, finding those sneaky New Zealand-isms and picking up the slack at home.

If you liked Murder for a Song, please consider reviewing it on Amazon or Goodreads. Every review helps!

ABOUT THE AUTHOR

Kim Jackways is a freelance writer and mother, based in New Zealand. She loves shady green places and teaching animals to talk. Her stories detail imaginary worlds filled with magic, with main characters who are somehow smarter and funnier than her.

www.ingramcontent.com/pod-product-compliance
Lightning Source LLC
Chambersburg PA
CBHW021151110726

47900CB00002B/516